FRIEND
or
FOE

WHICH SIDE ARE YOU ON?

BRIAN GALLAGHER

THE O'BRIEN PRESS
DUBLIN

First published 2015 by The O'Brien Press Ltd,
12 Terenure Road East, Rathgar, Dublin 6, D06 HD27, Ireland.
Tel: +353 1 4923333; Fax: +353 1 4922777
E-mail: books@obrien.ie
Website: www.obrien.ie
Reprinted 2015, 2016 (twice).

ISBN: 978-1-84717-631-8

8 7 6 5 4
18 17 16

Printed and bound by CPI Group (UK) Ltd, Croydon, CR0 4YY

The paper in this book is produced using pulp from managed forests.

DEDICATION

To the Halpin and Kelly families – great cousins.

And in memory of Mary Webb, a great editor.

ACKNOWLEDGEMENTS

My sincere thanks to Michael O'Brien for supporting the idea of a novel that would cover the Easter Rising from a different angle; to my editor, Nicola Reddy, for her skilful editing and advice; to publicist Ruth Heneghan for all her efforts on my behalf; to Emma Byrne for her excellent design work; and to everyone at The O'Brien Press, with whom, as ever, it's a pleasure to work.

I'm grateful to Cliona Fitzsimons for her support, and to Connor Kelly, Emer Geisser and Ciara Fitzsimons, three young readers who shared with me their views of an early draft of the story.

My thanks also go to Hugh McCusker for his painstaking proof-reading, and to Amy Brogan for allowing me to examine the interior of her house on Ardmore Avenue. The subject matter of this book is still sensitive for some people, and any errors, artistic licence or opinions expressed are mine and mine alone.

And finally, the greatest thanks of all go to my family, Miriam, Orla and Peter, for all their support and encouragement.

PROLOGUE

**EASTER MONDAY, APRIL 24TH, 1916
CHURCH STREET, DUBLIN**

Emer was thrilled to be on a mission. She made her way towards the General Post Office, her heart racing with excitement. She concentrated hard on walking casually, not wanting to arouse suspicion if she encountered the police or an army patrol. In truth, though, there was little normal about today, and already she had experienced the most dramatic events of her life. History was being made in Ireland, and she was part of it.

Her father was a part-time officer in the Irish Volunteers, but Dad would be horrified if he knew that she was playing a role in today's uprising against the British. Although she was twelve years old now, her parents were protective; it was one of the drawbacks to being an only child. But Emer was willing to take whatever punishment came her way later on – she simply had to be involved in today's events.

Despite the warm spring sunshine, she had felt goose bumps when she saw an Irish tricolour flag tied to a lance that was wedged into the roadway. She had heard people on a street corner saying that the rebels at the Four Courts had clashed with British cavalry, and that the Lancers had beaten a hasty retreat – a story that seemed to be confirmed by the captured lance serving as a makeshift flagpole.

Now as she walked down Church Street with a secret rebel report in her cardigan pocket, there was a tang in the air from the nearby Jameson's distillery. She planned to avoid the British Army barracks at the Linen Hall and the police station at the Bridewell by cutting down Mary's Lane. It seemed incredible to Emer that in the space of one day Dublin had gone from being a peaceful city to a place of turmoil, with explosions, gunfire, cavalry charges and the other trappings of war.

But while the rebels regarded themselves as soldiers fighting a justified war, and were dressed in uniforms, she was playing her role in civilian clothes. Would that make her a spy in the eyes of the British? The thought was frightening – spies were routinely executed. *No!* decided Emer. *I can't think like that or I'll lose my nerve.*

She turned into Mary's Lane and headed towards Capel Street. She knew this part of the city well and had often visited the nearby market, where her father bought the supplies for his fruit and vegetable shops. Thinking of Dad, she hoped that he was all right. Emer had no doubt that he would fight bravely with his fellow rebels, yet part of her didn't want him to be too heroic.

Before she could think about it any further, she stopped dead at the sudden appearance of a patrol of British soldiers. The troops turned a corner near the market and began crossing Mary's Lane.

There were seven or eight of them, and they carried rifles with bayonets attached. One soldier, who was wounded in the leg, was being helped by two of his comrades.

Emer realised that she shouldn't have stopped on seeing them, and so she moved again now, making for the other side of the road.

'Oi, where are you going?' cried a voice.

Emer kept walking briskly, as though she hadn't heard. She hoped that, with a wounded comrade to deal with, the soldiers might let her go.

'You there! Halt!'

The order was shouted in a harsh English accent, and this time Emer had no choice but to stop, her heart thumping in her chest.

'Get back here!' cried the man, and Emer turned and retraced her steps towards the soldiers.

'She's only a kid, Corp,' said one of them.

'Kids can act as runners,' answered the corporal, his eyes boring into Emer as she stopped in front of him.

The man had a boxer's crooked nose and cold, hard eyes, and Emer felt her stomach tightening in fear. *Stay cool*, she told herself. *Act as though you're completely innocent.*

'Where do you think you're going?'

'I'm visiting my granny, Corporal,' answered Emer politely.

'There's a bleedin' war goin' on, and you visit your granny?'

'I wanted to make sure she's OK. She lives on Mary Street, near the GPO, where all the trouble is,' answered Emer, surprised at how readily the lie came.

The soldier was staring at her, and Emer wasn't sure whether or not she had convinced him.

'What's your name?'

On instinct Emer gave a false name. 'Gladys Clarke,' she replied, combining the first name of her best friend and the surname of her teacher.

'Gladys Clarke, eh?

'Yes, Corporal.'

'OK, Gladys, be on your way.'

Emer tried hard not to let her relief show. 'Thank you.'

She could see that the leg of the wounded soldier behind the corporal was soaked in blood. He looked young and frightened and was obviously in pain, and as Emer prepared to leave, she felt sorry for him – even if he was the enemy.

'But before you go,' said the corporal, 'turn out your pockets for me.'

Emer felt her blood run cold, but she tried not to panic. 'Look, I haven't done anything wrong,' she said, trying to sound reasonable, 'and I really want to check on my granny. Can I just go, please?'

'When I say you can.'

'We need to get Alf to a doctor, Corp,' said one of the other soldiers, and Emer prayed that taking care of his comrade would be more important to the corporal than searching her.

'Alf will be fine. But you won't be,' he added threateningly to Emer, 'if you don't empty your pockets.'

Emer desperately tried to think up some objection, but before she could, the soldier's patience ran out.

'Now!' he snapped.

'OK,' she answered, taking coins and a handkerchief out of the pockets of her dress, then turning the pockets themselves inside out. 'All right?' she asked.

'Now the cardigan.'

'Look, I really—'

'The cardigan!'

Emer's eyes darted about. She was desperate for any avenue of escape, knowing that the rebel report would be found in her cardigan pocket. The corporal grabbed her collar and roughly pulled the garment off her.

Emer swallowed hard, aware of what was coming. The soldier quickly rifled through the pockets, then found the folded piece of paper.

'Well, what have we here?' He swiftly read the sheet, then lowered it. 'I bloody sensed it!' he said, drawing closer to Emer. 'I bloody *knew* it!'

Even though she was terrified, Emer forced herself to stand her ground.

'Little Fenian bitch!' the man said, quickly striking out with his hand.

Emer reeled backwards, the smack taking her full in the face and knocking her off balance. She was shocked and her face stung badly, but she bit her lip, determined not to cry.

'You'll have some questions to answer back in the Linen Hall!'

said the corporal, grabbing Emer and pushing her ahead. 'OK, lads, let's get Alf to a sawbones.'

Emer moved in a daze as the patrol crossed Mary's Lane and continued north towards Linen Hall Barracks. She could feel her limbs trembling, but she tried to think clearly. In about five minutes they would reach their destination. She shuddered to imagine her fate when they got to the barracks; somehow she had to get away before then. But how? The one advantage she had was that she knew intimately the warren of streets between the vegetable market and the barracks, and if she could just break away she might well shake off her pursuers. The soldiers were also slowed down and distracted by the wounded trooper.

Was there any other trick she could use? Yes, she decided, she could give the impression of being defeated so that they might pay less attention to her. 'I'm sorry, Corporal,' she said, feigning tears. 'I didn't mean to cause trouble.'

'Should have thought of that before now!' snapped the soldier.

'What will happen to me?' asked Emer, with a sob in her voice.

'Same as all the other traitors who've stabbed our lads in the back!' said the corporal. 'Now shut it till we get to the barracks!'

Emer snivelled and walked on with her head down. She reckoned that she had fooled the corporal into thinking her a thoroughly broken opponent, but to take advantage of it she had to act soon. They came to the junction with Cuckoo Lane, and the wounded soldier cried out in pain as he lost his footing on the smooth curve of the cobblestones.

'It's OK, mate, we have you!' said one of his comrades, tightening his grip on the grimacing soldier.

'Hold on to the lads and take the weight off your leg,' instructed the corporal.

For a moment all the attention was on the injured soldier, and Emer realised that she mightn't get a chance like this again. She felt paralysed with fear, knowing that if she ran away she might end up with a bullet in the back. But being held prisoner and interrogated was terrifying too, and Emer willed herself to be brave.

The corporal was tightening a rough tourniquet around the wounded soldier's leg. Emer took a deep breath and forced herself to act. She backed away slightly then suddenly turned and sprinted down Cuckoo Lane. She tried to keep her first steps really light, to gain as much ground as possible before the soldiers realised that she was fleeing. She heard a cry behind her, then the corporal shouted, 'Plug her!'

A shot rang out and Emer accelerated, sheer terror fuelling her speed. Up ahead was the junction with Halston Street. If she could get round the corner she might be able to hide in the church, or escape into the nearby side streets. *If she could get round the corner.*

She zigzagged, trying to make herself a harder target. Another shot rang out, and the bullet ricocheted off the cobblestones at her feet. Her pounding heart felt like it would explode, but still the corner of Halston Street loomed ahead. Emer frantically sprinted towards it, approaching the junction just as a murderous volley of shots was unleashed by the soldiers.

PART ONE

BUILD-UP

CHAPTER ONE

JULY 1915

TOLKA VALLEY, DUBLIN

Three weeks into the summer holidays, Jack Madigan came face to face with death. It was a beautiful sunny day and all the Ellesmere gang had walked the two miles from Ellesmere Avenue to their swimming haunt on the River Tolka. There was Jack, Ben Walton and his sister Gladys, Joan Lawlor and Emer Davey.

There had been nothing to suggest that it would be anything other than another happy summer day. They had pretended to walk the plank when crossing the lock on the Royal Canal near Broom Bridge, placed a halfpenny on the track of the Great Western line and had it flattened by a passing train, and sung along when Jack led them in the lively music hall song 'Any Old Iron'. Even Ben's bitter complaint about the Football Association – which had decided there would be no international soccer next season because of the continuing war between Britain and Germany – hadn't dampened their spirits.

While crossing Ballyboggan Road Emer had used the melting tar to smear her initials onto a kerbstone, and even though he disapproved slightly, Jack hadn't objected, not wanting to spoil the mood. As the son of a policeman Jack had inherited his father's deep respect for keeping the law. Emer, on the other hand, had a father who was a member of the anti-government Irish Volunteers. She also had a headstrong streak, which Jack's mother said was indulged because she was an only child. Nevertheless Jack liked Emer and usually avoided conflict with her.

Leaving Ballyboggan Road behind, they had made their way to the swimming hole on the River Tolka. Joan Lawlor led the run to the water's edge before jumping in with her usual cry of 'Gang way!' Despite the summer heat, the river was chilly, and after a few minutes various members of the gang began to swim to the grassy bank and climb out.

Jack had been the last to make for the bank and had drifted a little downstream from the others when he got into trouble. He had been swimming for about a year and had never had a problem before. Unlike Emer, who was a brilliant swimmer, Jack didn't like immersing his face when he swam, but he had developed a version of the crawl that was reasonably effective.

Now, though, as he went to kick his legs he found his right foot trapped. The unexpected pull on his leg disoriented him, and in crying out in surprise, he swallowed a mouthful of river water.

It had a reedy taste, and Jack immediately gagged. He kicked his right leg to free it, but the clump of weeds holding his foot didn't give way. He felt a surge of fear. Instinctively twisting his head to see what was trapping him, he swallowed more water and felt the horrible sensation of his stomach filling and liquid going up his nose. Losing his bearings, he thrashed about in panic and found his head submerged. He opened his eyes and could see sunlight filtering down through the water. His chest felt like it would burst, and he flailed about with his arms, desperate to break the surface and to gasp oxygen into his lungs.

His foot was still trapped, but sheer terror gave him strength. He kicked again, harder this time, and his trapped foot finally came free. But he wasn't out of trouble. Between his panic and the awful sensation of the water suffocating him, he was still disoriented and found it hard to surface.

Jack swallowed more water just as he broke through, and he gagged and felt himself going under again. He had already been tired from swimming when he decided to come ashore, and much of his remaining strength had been spent in the effort to free his foot and stay afloat. Desperately he tried to surface again, then suddenly there was a splashing alongside him, and he felt his head being pulled backwards.

Overwhelmed by the instinct to survive, he continued to struggle, even though his head had been pulled above the water.

'It's OK, Jack, I have you!'

Despite his confusion Jack was aware that it was Emer's voice, and he thrust out his hand, desperate for her help. He made contact with her arm and grasped it firmly.

'Don't pull me under, Jack!'

He felt Emer wrenching her hand free, and from the corner of his eye he saw her swimming around behind him. Sickened from all the water he had swallowed and gasping for oxygen, Jack couldn't think clearly. He flailed again, fearing that Emer had abandoned him to protect herself.

'It's OK, Jack!' she cried from behind him. 'I have you, just relax!'

He felt her hand grasping his jaw.

'Don't fight me, Jack, just relax!'

His head was spinning, but somehow he realised that he had to be brave. His every instinct was to clutch her for safety, yet that was the very thing that would put them both in peril. His strength was gone, his lungs ached and he was still spluttering, but Jack forced himself to do as his friend ordered and ceased flailing about.

'OK, Jack, I have you now!' said Emer. 'It's all right, that's good, that's good!'

Emer had a firm grip on his chin, and Jack felt himself being towed backwards as she swam towards the bank. Before he knew what was happening, his friends hauled first him and then Emer from the water onto the grassy slope.

'Roll him onto his stomach!' cried Emer, and before Jack could react he had been rolled over and Emer was pressing hard on his back. The pressure on his lungs was painful, but he suddenly expelled the water that he had swallowed. It was a horrible feeling, yet he felt the better for it. Emer sat back wearily on the grass and, still panting, Jack sat up shakily.

'Thanks, Emer,' he gasped. 'Thanks.'

'My God, Jack, that was touch and go.'

Jack was aware that he could have pulled her under and, still gasping, he looked at her apologetically. 'I'm sorry,' he managed to get out. 'I'm ... I'm really sorry for–'

'It's fine. Really, I wasn't complaining. I'm just glad you're alive.'

'Not as much as me,' answered Jack.

'I thought you were a goner!' said Joan, her eyes wide with the drama of it all.

'Thanks, Joan,' said Jack.

'No, like, I'm really glad you're not. Imagine having to tell your da!'

'If we were Arabs,' said Gladys seriously, 'Jack would be Emer's slave now.'

'What?' asked Ben, looking quizzically at his sister.

'I read in a book that if an Arab saves your life, then you owe him that life. Like you're his slave for the rest of your days.'

Jack's breathing was returning to normal now, and he looked at Gladys with a hint of amusement. 'Just as well we're not Arabs then.'

'Pity though,' said Emer with a smile. 'I wouldn't mind having a slave!'

Jack returned her smile, then spoke seriously. 'I won't forget this, Emer. I owe you a big favour. Anything you ever want – just ask. Is that a deal?'

Emer looked at him. 'OK,' she said. 'That's a deal.'

CHAPTER TWO

Any excuse was a good excuse, Emer felt, when it came to interrupting piano practice. It wasn't that she had anything against playing, as such, and if she could have done popular tunes like 'Swanee River' or 'You Made Me Love You', practising might almost have been enjoyable. Instead her mother sent her for lessons with Miss Gildea, who lived around the corner from Ellesmere Avenue in a tall house on the North Circular Road. Miss Gildea slapped her pupils on the knuckles with a wooden ruler, and insisted that the correct piano music for young ladies was by Chopin, Beethoven and Liszt.

Emer had been working her way through a Chopin prelude in the parlour when there was a knock on the front door. She was glad to hear Jack politely greeting her mother, then Mam ushering him into the hall. Her mother did the book-keeping for Dad's greengrocer shops and would sometimes complain about being distracted if too many of Emer's friends called to the door when she was going through the invoices. Mam liked Jack the best of all her friends, however, and had returned his greeting warmly.

It was strange, really, because both of Emer's parents were wary of Jack's father, Mr Madigan. He was a pleasant, friendly man, but he was also a sergeant in the Dublin Metropolitan Police and therefore an agent of the government. At present, Ireland was ruled from London. Emer's father and mother were nationalists: they wanted, at the very minimum, a change to Home Rule – which would mean a parliament in Dublin to deal with local affairs. For preference, though, they wanted an independent Irish republic and a complete break with British rule. Her father, in particular, was on a collision course with the government since he had joined the Irish Volunteers. All of their parents were still very polite to each other as neighbours, but Dad had warned Emer not to discuss the family's politics with Jack. *As if Jack would snitch back to his father*, Emer thought – although she hadn't actually said that to Dad.

Now Mam opened the parlour door. 'Jack to see you, Emer.'

'Aw no,' said Emer playfully, 'just when I'm practising Chopin.'

'If you'd rather practise, I can call back,' said Jack with a grin.

'Well, let's not be hasty!'

Mam smiled. 'I'll leave the pair of you to it,' she said, closing the parlour door and returning to her book-keeping.

'So?' said Emer, swinging around on her piano stool. 'How are you feeling?'

'OK. But yesterday was pretty scary.'

'Yeah,' agreed Emer. 'When I thought about it last night I got the shivers.'

'Me too. And I know I thanked you at the time, but I wanted to say thanks properly. So I got you something.'

'There was no need, Jack. But what is it?' she added.

He reached into his pocket. 'Nothing much. I got my pocket

money today, and I know you like jellies, so here.' He handed over a bag of sweets.

'Thanks, Jack,' replied Emer. Although the conversation was light-hearted, she was touched by his gesture. She held out the bag, and they each had a sweet, then she looked thoughtful. 'I was thinking last night ...' she said.

'Yeah?'

'Remember you said how great it was that I knew life-saving? Well, why don't you join my swimming club? Then you could become a better swimmer – even go on to life-saving if you wanted?'

Jack looked thoughtful. 'In one way I'd love to.'

'So what's the problem?'

'I'm not ...' Jack looked a little sheepish. 'I know it sounds stupid, but I'm not great at putting my face down into the water. And good swimmers have to.'

'Sure I usen't to like that either,' said Emer. 'But they teach you how to do it. Really, it's not that hard when you're taught right.'

'It's not just that. There's my da as well. If I wanted to join a swimming club he might be suspicious and wonder why I'm asking now. And I *really* don't want him to know what happened yesterday.'

'Right.' Emer chewed on her jelly, savouring the sugary taste as she considered Jack's situation. 'There might be a way round that,' she suggested.

'How?'

'The Old Reliable, I call it.'

Jack breathed out. 'OK, I'll ask. What's the Old Reliable?'

'It's what nearly always sways parents. You tell them that the other parents have agreed to something. Then once that's persuaded them, your friend tells his or her parents that *your* parents have agreed. Works really well.'

Jack laughed. 'It's not bad.'

'Know how we make it even better?'

'No, how?'

'We get the Waltons to join as well. You talk to Ben, I'll talk to Gladys. Everyone tells their parents that all the other parents have agreed, and the Old Reliable does the trick!'

'Do you think Ben and Gladys would be on for that?'

'Yeah, Gladys was dead impressed with my life-saving yesterday, and sure Ben thinks you're great.'

'You know … that might actually work.'

'What am I?' asked Emer.

Jack pretended to consider the answer. 'Bossy, headstrong, spoiled rotten …'

Emer punched him playfully. 'A genius, is the answer you're looking for!' She opened the bag of sweets and offered Jack another jelly. 'So, will we give it a try?'

'Yeah, why not?'

'Great,' said Emer, then she popped a sweet into her mouth, swung round on the stool and loudly banged out a dramatic chord on the piano.

'Don't be such a snob, Ma!'

'I'm not,' said Jack's mother, looking up from her embroidery. 'I'm just saying you don't want to get in with the wrong crowd in that factory.'

Jack sat in a corner of the kitchen as his sisters Una and Mary argued with Ma about going on a day trip with the other staff of the munitions factory where they worked. At twelve years of age, Jack was the youngest in the family, with four sisters. His eldest sister, Sheila, was a milliner like Ma, and Maureen worked in a shop in town. Una and Mary had grasped the opportunity presented by the war and were earning good money in a factory that produced artillery shells.

Jack half listened now as his mother cautioned Una and Mary about not associating too much with some of the rougher workers. He liked this time, late in the evening, when the family gathered together, even if sometimes there were arguments and different family members were engaged in their own pursuits. Jack himself was following his hobby of fretwork, sawing an intricate pattern around the border of a piece of wood. Sheila and Maureen were out at a concert, and his father read the newspaper as he relaxed in his favourite armchair beside the fireplace.

Jack wanted to ask Da about joining the swimming club, and he had decided to use Emer's 'Old Reliable' tactic when the time seemed right. The near-drowning had actually shaken him up more than he had admitted to his friends, and he was determined to become a better swimmer – and maybe even get a chance to rescue a life in return for his own – by learning life-saving. Before he got the chance to pitch the idea to his father, however, Da lowered the newspaper and spoke.

'My God, it's turning into a slaughter.'

'What is, Da?' asked Jack.

'This war with Germany. They've released casualty figures. Three hundred and thirty thousand casualties since last August.'

To Jack, this sounded like a staggeringly high number of people, but the war – which people had said would be over by the previous Christmas – still showed no signs of ending. Russia and France were allied with the British Empire, but Germany and the Austro-Hungarian Empire were united on the other side along with Turkey, where Jack's uncle Bertie was fighting in a place called the Dardanelles.

'That's an awful lot of people, Da,' answered Jack.

'It is, son. More than every single man, woman and child on the northside of Dublin.'

Somehow this made the numbers seem more real, and Jack was horrified. He remembered thinking at first that the war was a great adventure, like in the books he read. He had been proud of his mother's brother Bertie, a Ringsend man who was in the Dublin Fusiliers, a famous regiment in the British Army, and of Mam's nephew Ronnie from Manchester, who had volunteered at the outbreak of war and was serving in Belgium. Now, though,

Jack felt almost guilty about his earlier attitude, and he prayed every night that his relations would come home in one piece, and that the war would end.

'Do you think we'll win soon, Da?' he asked.

His father breathed out wearily. Usually Da was optimistic, but now his tone was cautious. 'I'd love to say yes, Jack. But both sides are bogged down on the Western Front.'

Jack knew that the Western Front was the blood-soaked line of trenches that ran for hundreds of miles through Belgium and France.

'And when we get the upper hand somewhere like Africa,' Da continued, 'they get on top someplace else like Turkey.'

'Right.'

As though aware of his downbeat manner, his father raised his chin and spoke more hopefully. 'Still, huge numbers of Irishmen have shown loyalty to the Crown by joining up. That should count for something when the Home Rule Bill is reviewed after the war.'

John Redmond, the leader of the Irish Party at Westminster, had urged Irishmen who wanted Home Rule to fight for Britain in her hour of need. But although Jack approved of thousands of Irishmen joining up, part of him was glad that Da was a policeman and safely stationed in Dublin. Even if they brought in conscription – forcing men to join the army to make up for all the losses – his father's age and job probably meant that he wouldn't be sent off to the front.

'Still, the war isn't all bad, Da,' said Una now, turning away from Ma and the argument about not mixing with girls from the factory. 'I know it's terrible about the killing and all,' she continued, 'but the war's brought loads of work. Plenty of people who were going hungry are earning a living now.'

'There is that,' conceded Da.

Jack hadn't thought of it that way before, and Una did have a point. *But still.* Thousands of people were being killed and maimed; there had to be better ways of creating jobs than by countries going to war.

Just then Sheila and Maureen arrived home from their concert, and the conversation moved in a different direction. Normally Jack would have been keen to hear about the latest music hall songs, but all this talk of war and his own near-drowning had made him realise that life was fragile, and he continued quietly with his sawing, lost in his thoughts.

He had to approach Da about the swimming club. But the mood wasn't right tonight, and it would be better to wait than to waste his chance through ill timing. A little disappointed, Jack concentrated on his fretwork, resolving to make his move the minute the time was right.

CHAPTER THREE

Emer felt slightly guilty. She was sitting in the sun on the kerb outside her house on Ardmore Avenue with Gladys, and had just persuaded her to join the swimming club. It was typical of Gladys to be agreeable, even if before now she had shown no great interest in improving as a swimmer. Emer didn't like manipulating her, but she told herself that it would be in Gladys's and Ben's interest to be better swimmers.

Jack and Ben were round the corner in the Waltons' house on Glenard Avenue, and with Joan Lawlor away visiting her granny, Emer had grasped the opportunity to get Gladys on her own. 'You can tell your parents that I'll look out for you and that Jack is joining too,' said Emer now, wanting to reassure her friend.

'OK,' agreed Gladys, 'I'll say that to Mam.'

'Great.'

'Ah, here come the boys,' said Gladys as Jack and Ben came down the lane in good spirits.

'Close your eyes and open your mouth, and see what God will send you!' Ben said to Emer. She hesitated, knowing the mischief that Jack and Ben sometimes got up to, but Gladys spoke reassuringly.

'It's OK. We got you something on our day trip yesterday.'

'Some day trip,' said Ben as he and Jack sat down on the kerb. 'Dad said it would be a surprise, and I was sure it would be the seaside – somewhere good, like Bray.'

'The Meeting of the Waters is still nice,' said Gladys.

'Two measly rivers joining forces,' snorted Ben. 'If Tom Moore hadn't written a song about it, who'd even go there?!'

'Anyway, give Emer her souvenir,' said Gladys.

'Is it a stick of rock?'

'That would be telling,' answered Jack. 'You have to close your eyes and open your mouth, like Ben said.'

'This better not be a worm or something,' Emer warned, then she did as she was bid.

She felt something hard and round being slipped into her mouth, and she opened her eyes in alarm. The others all laughed, and Emer realised that it was a shiny black stick of liquorice.

'They didn't sell sticks of rock,' explained Gladys, 'so you'll have to settle for that.'

'It's great,' said Emer. 'Liquorice lasts for ages, and I love the way it makes your teeth look like they're rotten! Thanks, Ben, thanks, Gladys.'

'You're grand,' said Ben.

'Did Gladys tell you the comedian's jokes from yesterday?' asked Jack.

'No,' answered Emer.

'Sure I'm no good at telling jokes,' said Gladys.

'Neither was the comedian,' said Ben.

'Neither are you. All you're good at is cricket,' said Gladys.

'At least I'm good at something,' retorted Ben to his sister, before turning to the others. 'We ran into a Works Outing yesterday,' he said, 'and this fella from the company was telling all these fish jokes — just because they were at the Meeting of the Waters.'

'Like what?' queried Emer.

'Like … what's the best way to catch a fish?' asked Ben.

'What is?'

'Have someone throw it at you!'

'That's not bad,' said Emer. 'And talking about water and swimming …' She looked enquiringly at Jack, who gave her a thumbs-up.

'We talked it over,' he said. 'Ben's on for joining the club.'

'Great!' said Emer. 'Gladys is too, aren't you, Glad?'

'Yeah.'

'So we can all be in it together,' said Emer. 'I'll ask Joan too when she comes back from her granny's.'

'So we each hit our parents with the Old Reliable then?' asked Jack.

Ben frowned. 'What's the Old Reliable?'

'Emer's trick for winning over parents,' answered Jack. 'Will you explain it, or will I?'

'You tell them,' said Emer smilingly. 'I want to stuff my face!' Then she broke off a length of the liquorice and slipped it into her mouth, pleased at how things were working out.

'You're in trouble with Da!' Jack's sister Mary was unable to keep the glee out of her voice as she entered the kitchen.

'Why?'

'You tell me. But he wants to talk to you in the parlour, and he looks dead annoyed. I wouldn't like to be you.'

'It'd be worse being you!' snapped Jack. Mary was the youngest of his sisters and although sixteen now, four years older than Jack, she could still be childish. She claimed that he was spoiled, but he didn't think he was, and sometimes – like now – he found her really annoying.

Before Mary could think of a retort, Jack made for the hall, then stopped outside the parlour. Da sometimes retreated there when he wanted to do police paperwork without interruption or play his violin. It was also the room, however, to which he occasionally summoned family members for a talking-to. Jack hesitated, then nervously tapped on the door.

'Come in.'

Jack took a breath to steady himself and stepped into the parlour. His mind was racing as he tried to figure out what might have him in trouble.

'Sit down, Jack. We need to talk,' said Da.

Jack studied his father's face, unsure if Mary had been exaggerating or telling the truth about him being annoyed. He certainly looked serious, but his voice didn't sound furious.

Jack sat in an armchair, then looked at Da, whose big frame completely filled the opposite armchair. He hadn't seen much of his father in the last couple of days – there had been a serious incident in A Division of the DMP – and he hadn't yet had the chance to ask about joining the swimming club. And now that he was in trouble, once again the time wouldn't be right.

'Is there anything you want to tell me?' asked Da.

Jack shook his head. 'No, Da.'

His father continued in a calm voice. 'When you grow up you want to be a policeman like me, don't you?'

Jack had read all the Sherlock Holmes stories, and it was his dream to be a detective rather than a uniformed sergeant like Da. But he didn't want to hurt his father's feelings, so he simply answered, 'Yes'. He had no idea where the conversation was going, but he forced himself to concentrate as his father continued.

'To be a policeman you have to be trained in drill, and observation, and how to give evidence. You have to learn the geography of the city, the correct way to patrol, the handbook of police regulations. But the most important thing is integrity. You must be honest and straight-forward in all your dealings.'

Jack nodded, sensing that he was being charged with dishonesty but still unsure of what he had done.

'Honesty isn't just *not lying*,' said Da. 'Sometimes saying nothing about what's happened is a form of dishonesty. Do you see what I'm getting at?'

'I … I think so, Da. But I'm not sure what I did wrong.'

'You put me in a position where I felt like a fool. Mr Lawlor sympathised with me over the fright you must have gotten when you nearly drowned – and I had no idea what he was talking about.'

Joan Lawlor and her big mouth! thought Jack. *Wait till I see her!*

'You should have told me that Emer Davey saved you from drowning. I shouldn't have heard it from a neighbour.'

'I'm sorry, Da, I …'

'You what?'

Jack hesitated. 'I was afraid if I told you I'd get in trouble.'

'Why would you get in trouble? Were you trick-acting in the water?'

'No! No, my foot got caught in weeds or something and I swallowed water, and all of a sudden I was in trouble.'

'So why didn't you just tell me that?'

'I don't know,' answered Jack, then he remembered Da's instruction to be completely honest. He sighed before continuing. 'Maybe … maybe I was afraid you'd ban me from swimming in the river. And I love it. We've great fun when we all go up there.'

His father said nothing.

'I'm really sorry I put you on the spot with Mr Lawlor, Da. I … I suppose I didn't think it all through.'

'You certainly didn't!'

Jack looked at his father nervously. Da was a reasonable man and not easily given to anger, but once he decided something there was no swaying him. Would he ban swimming trips to the

Tolka now as a punishment? Or, if not as a punishment, then as a safety measure?

'As a policeman, Jack, I have a certain standing,' said Da. 'That gets undermined if I'm made to look foolish – so I can't have that. Do you understand?'

'Yes, Da.'

'So, what would you do if you were me?'

This was a question that Da often asked, though usually it was about police matters, as a way of preparing Jack for the day when he too entered the force. Jack thought carefully, and the germ of an idea sprouted in his mind.

'I'd do what you've just done, Da,' he answered, 'and explain it like you have – so now I'll know to be more honest in future. And, eh … the other thing I'd do …'

'Yes?'

Jack gathered his nerve, then spoke. 'The other thing I'd do is to see that I became a better swimmer. Joan and Ben and Gladys are all asking their parents to send them to Emer's swimming club. If I were you, I'd send me too. That way, if we all get trained, we'll be much safer in future when we go swimming.'

His father looked him in the eye, and Jack wondered if he had pushed his luck.

'So you don't think I should punish you?'

'I didn't *deliberately* do anything wrong, Da,' said Jack nervously.

His father seemed to consider this, and Jack prayed that he wouldn't be banned from the swimming hole.

Suddenly Da nodded. 'All right then. We'll leave it at that.'

Jack felt a flood of relief but decided to go for broke. 'And, eh … the swimming club?'

'Well, if all the others are joining, you'd better learn too.'

Jack wanted to shout with joy. Instead he kept his voice normal and smiled at his father.

'Thanks, Da. You're … you're a great da!'

'Less of your aul' *plámás*,' said his father, but there was a twinkle in his eye. 'Be off with you now, before I change my mind.'

'OK!' said Jack, then he grinned at his father and made for the door.

CHAPTER FOUR

'There's a boy over there staring at us,' said Gladys.

'Where?' asked Joan.

'Over there in the trees.'

'Let him,' said Emer. 'Sure aren't we worth staring at?!'

They were having a picnic under a cloudless sky on the grassy banks of the Tolka at the swimming hole. Today there were just the three girls, with Jack and Ben away at a football match. Emer had been listening to Joan tell of how her despairing violin teacher had given up on her and called round to her father. *'I can't take your money any more, Mr Lawlor, there's no point!'* Joan had mimicked.

Emer sometimes found Joan a bit silly, but she could be entertaining too, and Emer had been enjoying the story when Gladys had interjected that the boy was watching them. Now the rest of the anecdote was forgotten as the boy stepped out from the trees and began to approach.

'He's coming straight for us,' said Gladys.

'Relax,' said Emer. 'I think it's that boy that Jack knows.'

The three friends watched as the figure came closer, and Emer realised that it was indeed the schoolmate of Jack's. Sometimes the boy had spoken to Jack when they were all at the swimming hole.

He had never joined their group, however, and Jack had never introduced him, simply mentioning once that he knew him from school.

As the boy drew near Emer could see that his clothes were worn and tatty, and he had a look that her mother would describe as 'rough'.

'Howayis?' he said in a strong Dublin accent.

The three girls politely returned his greeting, then the boy cocked his head to one side. 'You're friends of Jack Madigan, aren't you?' he asked.

'Yes,' answered Emer, 'but he couldn't come with us today.'

'OK.'

There was a short pause, then Emer remembered her manners. 'I'm Emer,' she said, 'and this is Joan and Gladys.'

'Right,' said the boy.

Emer waited for him to introduce himself, then realised that he wasn't going to.

'And what's your name?'

'Gerry.'

'Well, Gerry, it's nice to meet you,' she said.

He gave a brief nod of acknowledgement, then spoke haltingly. 'I was, eh … I was wondering …'

'Were you?' said Joan cheekily. 'About what?'

'If you might like to swap. Some of your picnic for apples I have.'

'No, thanks,' said Gladys.

'They're good apples.'

'I'm sure they are,' said Joan. 'But I'd rather have my sandwiches and cake.'

'They're really juicy, and I'd give you a good swap.'

'I don't care if the juice is running out of them,' answered Joan. 'I'm not swapping my lunch.'

'All right,' said the boy, and Emer sensed that he was trying to hide his disappointment.

Now that he was up close, she could see that beneath his shabby clothes he had a lean, wiry build. Emer realised that he might be one of the thousands of hungry people in Dublin who struggled every day to get enough to eat. 'OK, Gerry,' she said. 'I wouldn't mind a few juicy apples. What would I get for a chicken sandwich and a piece of lemon cake?'

Emer could see that her friends were taken aback, but she ignored them and looked instead into the eyes of the ragged boy. She had expected him to look pleased, but his face gave nothing away.

'I'll give you four apples,' he said.

Emer suspected that Gerry's lack of pleasure at her offer was a tactic and that he was someone who had to bargain hard for everything. She hesitated, trying to think on her toes. She didn't actually want the fruit, but she thought he looked hungry and she felt sorry for him. 'How about six apples?' she suggested, deciding that the best way to prevent it looking like charity was to bargain a bit.

He shook his head. 'Too much.'

'Supposing I throw in a biscuit as well?'

He considered, then nodded. 'With the biscuit, we could split the difference. I'll give you five apples – big, juicy ones.'

'OK,' said Emer. 'Done!'

'I have them up at the cottage,' said Gerry, indicating a ram-shackle building in the distance. 'Back in two minutes.'

'Fine,' said Emer as he abruptly turned on his heel and made off up the slope of the valley.

'Are you mad?' said Joan. 'Giving away half your lunch!'

'I'm not giving it away, I'm trading.'

'For five juicy apples!' said Joan, viciously taking off Gerry's flat Dublin accent.

'I don't think we should have anything to do with him,' said Gladys.

'Why not?' asked Emer.

'He's … well, he's …'

'What?'

'He's common, Emer. Our parents wouldn't want us talking to him. It looks like he lives in a shack.'

'Come on, Gladys. It's not a crime to be poor.'

'It's not a crime,' said Joan, 'but that doesn't mean we have to be his friend.'

'Did either of you think that maybe he's hungry?'

Gladys looked surprised. 'Is that why you swapped?'

'Yes. You don't think I really wanted the apples, do you?'

'If you don't eat them, and you give away half your lunch,' said Joan, '*you're* the one who'll be hungry.'

'Even if I am, I won't be hungry tonight when I have my

dinner. But maybe he will. And I won't be hungry tomorrow night either. But maybe he will then too.'

'Even so, Emer,' said Gladys, 'I don't think our parents would …'

'For God's sake, Gladys!'

'What?'

'There are babies dying, and children sick, and people starving all over Dublin. And you're worried about me giving a sandwich to a boy who's hungry – and what our parents might think!'

There was an uncomfortable silence, and Emer breathed deeply to dampen her irritation. Why could her friends not see that the world needed to be changed? That it *had* to be changed, so that nobody lived in shacks or went hungry? She rarely discussed politics with her friends, however, and now wasn't the moment to give them her theories. But she thought yet again that if Ireland became an independent republic, as Dad wanted, then there could be a new kind of country where everyone was looked after.

'Sorry, Emer,' said Gladys. 'You were just being kind.'

'It's OK. And I didn't mean to snap at you. But when he comes back with the apples, let's not be snooty, girls. All right?'

Gladys nodded. 'All right.'

'Joan?'

'I'll greet him like the Prodigal Son!'

They all laughed, and Emer was pleased that peace had been restored. Then she saw the approaching figure of Gerry in the distance, so she began wrapping up the agreed food, glad that she had done the right thing.

'Did you ever wonder what it's like being a cow?' asked Ben.

'No,' answered Jack with a laugh, 'I never, ever imagined myself as a cow!'

They were walking past the huge cattle market on the North Circular Road, with its pens full of lowing animals. The evening air was warm and scented with the smell of animals and fodder, and as they walked on Jack was amused that his normally sensible friend had come up with such an idea. Usually Ben was the least imaginative member of the gang – apart from his dream of being a professional cricketer – but tonight he was clearly in an inquisitive mood.

'What goes through their heads, do you think?' Ben continued. 'I mean, they're standing there all day eating grass – what are they thinking about?'

'Their next meal, probably!' suggested Joan. *Is the grass in this field going to run out? Is the farmer going to move us into the field with all the nettles?!'*

'Would you say that's all they think of?' persisted Ben.

'No,' answered Emer, 'the musical ones probably think it's a shame Chopin died so young!'

'You're all very smart,' said Ben good-humouredly as they left the cattle market behind, crossed the North Circular Road and entered Ellesmere Avenue.

Jack liked it when everyone was in good form like this, and

tonight had been particularly enjoyable. They had all sung the music hall comedy piece 'I'm Henry the Eighth, I Am' while queuing for a tram in town, having attended their second week of swimming lessons at Emer's club in the Tara Street Baths. Even after two lessons Jack felt that he had made real progress, and Gladys and Ben were enthusiastic too. Joan had been told off by the swimming coach for trick-acting in the pool, but even that had been entertaining, when she had accurately mimicked him afterwards on the upper deck of their home-bound tram.

Now Jack said goodnight to Emer and Joan, who both lived on Ellesmere Avenue. He had been a little surprised the previous week when Emer had told him about his classmate Gerry Quinn approaching the girls at the swimming hole. Emer had asked a lot of questions about him, and Jack had explained that Gerry's parents had died in an accident, after which he went to stay with his impoverished Uncle Pat, who lived in the ramshackle cottage near the Tolka. Gerry was a classmate rather than a friend, so Jack didn't know all the details, but he told Emer that he imagined Gerry preferred living with his uncle to being sent to an orphanage.

Jack thought it was sad that Gerry had approached virtual strangers looking for food, but his opinion of Emer had gone up when he heard that she had swapped part of her lunch. Poverty and wealth sat side by side in Dublin, and many comfortably off people hardened their hearts and looked away from the needy. All of Jack's friends had fathers who earned a good living: Mr Walton was an electrical contractor, Mr Davey a shopkeeper and Mr Lawlor a clerk in an insurance company. It was all the more reason to admire Emer, that despite her background she hadn't turned away from a boy like Gerry.

Jack reached his doorway and said goodbye to Gladys and Ben, with Ben bidding him farewell by bowling an imaginary cricket ball at him. Jack smiled, then entered the house. After swimming Ma usually gave him a biscuit and a glass of milk, but as soon as he entered the kitchen to put down his rolled-up towel and swimming togs, he encountered an argument in full spate. His mother and father were sitting at the table with Maureen, his twenty-year-old sister, who was visibly angry.

'I can't believe this!' said Maureen. 'It's so unfair!'

Jack was intrigued, and he discreetly sat in the corner.

'We don't mean to be hard on you, Maureen,' said Jack's mother. 'It's nothing personal against Tommy—'

'It's nothing personal?! You just want me to break it off with him!'

'Only if he persists in this foolishness with the Volunteers,' said Da.

Jack's mind raced. He liked Maureen's boyfriend, Tommy, a friendly young man who worked in the deliveries section of the city-centre store where Maureen was a sales assistant. But Tommy had joined the Irish Volunteers, and Jack wasn't surprised that this caused a problem for his father.

'I can't force Tommy to leave the Volunteers,' said Maureen.

'Then he can't come to this house,' answered Da, 'and you can't be seen with him.'

Jack watched as his sister went to argue, but Da held up his hand. 'You're a policeman's daughter, Maureen. You've had all the benefits that go with that, but there's a price as well. And a policeman's daughter can't be with someone in an illegal organisation.'

'But thousands of men have joined the Volunteers,' countered Maureen.

'That doesn't make it legal.'

'But they haven't been arrested.'

'The DMP is a police force. We don't make policy; that's the government's job.'

'The government didn't move against the Ulster Volunteer Force in Belfast,' said Maureen. 'So why would they move against the Volunteers here in Dublin?'

Even though Jack was sympathetic to his sister's plight, he thought this was a poor argument. The Ulster Volunteer Force had been formed to prevent Home Rule for Ireland by force of arms. The Irish Volunteers had been formed partly to counter-balance the UVF, but also to force Home Rule or even total independence for Ireland. It was naïve to think that the British government would be even-handed in dealing with the two organisations, one of which was for, and the other against, British rule.

'Forget the government!' said Da. 'They don't run this house – I do, along with your mother. And you can't be with someone who's mixed up with the Volunteers. I'm sorry, Maureen, but that's how it is.'

'Why is that how it is for *me*?' demanded Maureen. 'It's not how it is for Jack!'

Jack was taken aback, but before he could ask what Maureen was talking about, she pointed at him.

'Jack is friends with Emer Davey, and her father is in the Volunteers. How come that's not a problem?'

Jack was really surprised to be drawn into the row. His mother, however, immediately intervened.

'That's not the same thing at all, Maureen,' she said.

'How isn't it?'

'First of all, Jack's still a child. Second of all, he's known Emer since they were toddlers, but it's only recently that her father joined the Volunteers.'

'It's only recently that Tommy joined the Volunteers.'

'But Tommy is an adult making his own choices,' answered Ma reasonably. 'Emer is a child, and she's not responsible for what her father decides. It's completely different.'

Jack said nothing, aware that Emer shared her father's nationalist views, but also aware that this was not the time to say so.

'There's no more to be said, Maureen,' said Da. 'Nothing but violence and bloodshed will come out of the Volunteers. So either Tommy leaves them, or you break it off with him. And that's my final word.'

Jack knew that when Da said something was his final word,

there was no going back. Maureen obviously realised it too, for tears formed in her eyes and she rose from the chair and ran towards her bedroom.

Jack understood his father's thinking, but even though Maureen had tried to drag him into the argument, he still felt a bit sorry for her. His earlier high spirits had been banished, and his father's prediction that the Volunteer movement would end in bloodshed was disturbing. If trouble was coming, would he and Emer end up on opposite sides?

'Milk and a biscuit, Jack?' asked Ma, in what he felt was an attempt to restore normality.

'Yes, please,' he answered, but the good had gone out of the evening, and he worried about what lay ahead.

CHAPTER FIVE

Emer pounded out her favourite rebel ballad, 'A Nation Once Again', on the piano in the sitting room, and her parents sang along with her. She loved moments like this. A lot of the time Dad was busy with his grocery shops or out drilling with the Volunteers, and Mam spent many hours doing the book-keeping or helping out with local charities. Occasionally, though, they would have what Dad called a 'recital'. Emer would start with the classical pieces that Miss Gildea taught her, but it usually ended with a more relaxed sing-song, during which she was allowed to play a few popular songs.

Dad had a nice tenor voice, and tonight he had performed 'My Wild Irish Rose'. He had light-heartedly sung some of the lyrics to Mam, and the general atmosphere was affectionate and happy. Now was the time, Emer thought, to raise what might be a tricky topic. 'I was just wondering …' she said, looking from her mother to her father.

'What?' asked Mam.

'It's great that Irish people are starting to want independence. And I'm really proud of you, Dad, being an officer in the Volunteers and all ...'

'I'm waiting for the "but",' said Dad.

'But I'd like to be part of it too,' answered Emer.

'You are,' said Mam. 'You're a fluent Irish speaker, and you know Ireland's history and all the patriotic songs.'

'But that's *knowing* stuff, Mam. I want to *do* things.'

'Like what?'

'I'd like to join Na Fianna.' Na Fianna was a youth wing attached to the Irish Volunteers. As soon as she said the words, Emer saw her father's face grow serious.

'That's not possible, Emer,' he said.

'Why not?'

'It's not for girls.'

'Not so far. But couldn't we start a girls' section?'

'That's not going to happen,' said Dad.

'Why not? Paudie Maguire from Phibsboro is in Na Fianna, and he's an eejit. What can he do that I can't?'

'Really, Emer!' said her mother disapprovingly.

'What, Mam? What single thing is he better at than me?'

'That's not the point.'

'Well, what is the point?'

'You're a girl from a good family. Being in Na Fianna, it wouldn't be …'

Emer tried to keep her patience. 'Wouldn't be what, Mam?' she asked reasonably.

'It wouldn't be appropriate. It wouldn't be proper.'

Emer looked enquiringly at her mother. 'You want a revolution – but it must be *proper*?'

'Yes, dear, we must stay respectable.'

Dad nodded in agreement. 'We don't want the government writing off the Volunteers as thugs and ne'er-do-wells,' he said. 'That's why we must behave properly at all times. And involving young girls in the national struggle wouldn't be proper.'

Emer had been expecting an objection like this, and she had her answer ready. 'But Countess Markievicz is respectable. And she's one of the people who founded Na Fianna.'

'But she's an adult, Emer. You're twelve years old,' said her mother.

'I know, Mam. But the boys in Na Fianna aren't adults, are they? So how is it all right for them to be involved?'

'Well, actually, I'm not sure it *is* all right for them to be involved.'

Emer was surprised by her mother's answer, and she turned to her father. 'Dad?'

'I'm with Mam, Emer. I'm not comfortable with youngsters getting involved in the struggle.'

'Why not?'

'Because in future it mightn't only be drilling and marching. If the government tries to force conscription in Ireland, or if the Ulster Volunteers revolt against Home Rule, there'll be fighting. I don't want to see children – boys *or* girls – involved in that.'

Mam reached out and placed her hand gently on Emer's arm. 'We especially don't want our lovely daughter in harm's way. So please, dear, put this notion out of your head. All right?'

Emer felt frustrated, even though she knew that her parents

meant well. If there was going to be a battle ahead, however, and if youngsters were going to be involved in it, then she wanted to be one of them. But nothing would be gained by arguing any further tonight. *Better to go along with them for now,* she thought.

'All right?' repeated her mother.

'All right, Mam,' Emer answered. 'All right.'

'Do you know what I'd love?' asked Joan dramatically as she breathed in the sweet mountain air while climbing Ballymana Hill.

Jack looked at her. 'No, Joan, what would you love?'

'I'd love to be on a train that was derailed!'

'Are you mad?' asked Ben in disbelief.

The mail train from London's Euston Station had been derailed the previous weekend, and the newspapers were full of dramatic pictures and articles.

'It's awful that passengers were killed,' admitted Joan, 'but if you were on the train and you weren't hurt, it would be a brilliant adventure.'

'You're a nutcase, Joan,' said Ben.

'Yeah, I'd hate that,' said Gladys. 'This is adventure enough.' She indicated the hillside that the friends were climbing in the hot August sunshine, with the sweep of Dublin city stretched out far below them.

Emer had told them about a great hike she had done with her

family last summer, and they had all persuaded their parents to allow them to retrace the route on a day-long picnic. They had taken the Blessington steam tram at Parkgate Street and alighted near Jobstown, with the intention of climbing over Ballymana Hill, swimming in the River Dodder at Old Bawn and finally making their way home via Tallaght.

'Back me up, Emer,' said Joan now. 'Wouldn't derailing be good?'

'Might be if you'd no ticket and the inspector was about to nab you! Otherwise I'd rather get off at the station.'

Joan looked appealingly to Jack. 'You're my last hope, Jack,' she said playfully. 'Don't tell me you're chicken as well.'

'Of course not. If I'm on a ship I like it to sink, if I'm on a train I like it to derail, if I'm on a bike I like it to hit a brick wall!'

The others laughed, and Joan said, 'I give up!'

'Like Gladys says, this is adventure enough,' said Jack, a little out of breath as the steep climb finally brought them to a rolling plateau. 'So, where do we go now, Emer?' he asked. 'The trail seems to end.'

'There's no proper trail for a while, but if we go along by the forest eventually there's a track that brings you down to the valley near Stone Cross.'

'Are you sure you'll be able to find it?' asked Gladys.

Emer nodded confidently. 'Yeah, over the stile here and make for those trees in the distance.'

Jack let the others climb the stile, then he mounted it and looked east towards the city. The sky was clear blue, the air was scented with the smell of gorse, and far below Dublin shimmered in the heat. They had chosen one of the nicest days of the summer for their adventure, and he felt in good spirits now after a downbeat start to the day.

His father had the *Irish Independent* newspaper delivered each morning, and over breakfast today Jack had seen large advertisements for back-to-school supplies. He hated the way the uniform suppliers and schoolbook companies advertised their wares when it was still just the middle of August – it was like they were wishing away the summer that Jack already felt was too short. But more worrying than the ads had been an article about how the British Army's campaign at Gallipoli had stalled, with troops exhausted and casualties mounting. Jack had prayed that his uncle Bertie wasn't among the Dublin Fusiliers who had been killed or wounded, and that the British and Australian troops would eventually defeat the Turks and thus help end the war.

Jack had left his house a little dispirited, but the combination of the fine weather, the company of his friends and the prospect of an adventure in the countryside had lifted his mood, and now he happily followed the others across the sunlit plateau.

They were planning to stop for a picnic lunch, and Jack was looking forward to the freshly baked apple tart that his mother had packed with his sandwiches. The shade of the evergreen trees in the nearby forest would make the perfect place to rest and escape the midday sun, he thought. 'What about having lunch over at the trees?' he asked the others.

'Stopping to eat always sounds good,' agreed Joan.

'Yeah, I'm pretty tired,' said Gladys.

Emer nodded. 'All right. There's a nice little glade just ahead there.'

'OK,' said Ben. 'Let me scout it for Apaches!'

Ben pulled the reins of an imaginary horse and was about to set off when the air was rent with a volley of shots. The sound was so unexpected on the remote plateau that the friends were all startled. Before anyone could speak, more shots rang out. Ben turned to Jack. 'Is that rifle fire?'

Still recovering from the shock, Jack nodded slowly. 'I think so.'

Another volley of shots shattered the peace of the hillside, the sound a little closer this time. Jack realised that the firing was coming from inside the forest. Then a fourth round rang out, closer still, and Jack swallowed nervously. This sounded very like military manoeuvres, but the army had no firing range or training area here, which left just one likely explanation: *rebels*. Jack's pulse started to quicken at the thought that they had stumbled across Volunteers who were training in shooting and skirmishing. Upon hearing a man's voice calling out an order, Jack stared intently into the forest. There were more shots, much closer this time, and the five friends stood unmoving as a group of seven or eight men came running through the trees, heading in their direction.

'Jack,' said Gladys nervously.

'Do nothing!' replied Jack. 'Do nothing and say nothing!'

The men had seen them now. Their leader drew nearer, then

stopped and pointed his rifle at Jack. The other men followed his lead, coming to a halt and aiming their rifles. The leader had a cold, hostile look in his eyes. There was a really threatening air about him, and Jack found his mind racing wildly. What if these men didn't want witnesses to their manoeuvres? Or didn't want witnesses to what they looked like? They were all young and tough-looking, but Jack tried to convince himself that while the Volunteers might be preparing to fight the British, they would hardly kill innocent Irish children. Even so, the leader's stare was frightening, and his rifle was still pointed at Jack's chest. Nobody said anything for what was probably only seconds, but seemed like a lifetime to Jack. Then the leader snapped a command to his men.

'Carry on!' he said, still unmoving and still with his own rifle raised. The other men quickly lowered their weapons and began to move off at speed across the plateau. The leader kept his eyes locked on Jack's, then raised his finger and tapped his lips in a gesture that signified silence. Jack tried to hold his gaze but felt his pulse racing even faster when the man slowly drew his finger across his throat in a slitting gesture, pointed threateningly, then tapped his lips again. The message was clear – he was warning them not to say anything about the encounter.

From the corner of his eye Jack saw Emer nodding in agreement, but even though he was scared, he refused to acknowledge the man's threat. The man held his finger to his lips one last time and pointed threateningly at Jack. Still Jack made no response.

There was a stalemate for a couple of seconds, then suddenly the leader turned on his heel and made off after his men.

'Oh my God!' said Gladys, breathing out in relief.

'Janey,' said Joan, 'he looked mad!'

'What should we do?' asked Ben.

'Nothing,' said Emer, her voice a little shaky. 'Sure what would we do?'

'We could go to the nearest police station or RIC barracks,' suggested Jack.

'And inform on Volunteers?' said Emer.

'For God's sake, Emer, they threatened us!'

'I know, that wasn't very nice. But even if you wanted to, there's no point reporting them. It would take forever to get from here to Tallaght – they'd be long since gone.'

Jack realised that this was true, but he still felt uncomfortable ignoring what had happened.

'Look, there's no point letting it spoil our day out,' said Emer. 'So let's have our lunch and go for our swim and just enjoy ourselves. OK?'

Jack hesitated.

'Please, Jack.'

Jack looked at her, then nodded in agreement. As far as he was concerned this wasn't over, and he'd give a description of the men to his father tonight. But for now he could see Emer's point that there was nothing to be gained by spoiling the day. 'OK,' he said. 'OK, then.'

'Here, I've a good one for you,' said Ben as he sat basking in the afternoon sunshine on the banks of the River Dodder at Old Bawn. 'Why don't they let elephants swim in Tara Street Baths?'

'Why don't they?' asked Joan.

'Because they might let down their trunks!'

Gladys turned to her brother. 'That's a bit rude, Ben.'

'Yeah, but it's funny,' said Joan. 'Don't be a stick-in-the-mud, Glad.'

'I'm just saying,' protested Gladys.

Emer didn't want her friends to start squabbling, so she interjected. 'Here, I've another swimming joke, and it's not rude. Why did the teacher jump into the river?'

'Why?' asked Joan.

'She wanted to test the water!'

The others laughed, then Joan stood up. 'Talking of rivers, let's jump in again!'

'OK,' said Ben, and he and Gladys rose to join her.

'I think I'll just sit in the sun for a while,' said Jack.

Emer had wanted to talk to him alone, and this was her opportunity, so she turned to Joan. 'You go ahead, I'll follow you after a bit.'

Joan gave her usual cry of 'Gang way!' then jumped into the river. Ben and Gladys followed her in, and the three of them splashed about.

Emer was pleased at the progress her friends had made in the three weeks since they had joined her club. She turned to Jack. 'You've all done really well. You're swimming much better now.'

'Thanks. Getting the hang of the breathing really helped.'

'Right.' Emer looked at him, a little uncertain how to begin. 'Jack ...'

'Yeah?'

'You've been a bit quiet since ... since earlier with the gunmen.'

'Have I? Sorry I ... I didn't mean to—'

'It's OK. It's just ...'

'What?'

Emer hesitated. She really liked Jack, and they had become closer this summer since she had saved him from drowning. She was afraid that what she wanted to say might put their friendship at risk, but she felt she had to speak up. 'I know normally we don't talk about ... well, my dad being in the Volunteers and your dad being a policeman,' she began.

'There's no point,' answered Jack. 'Just 'cause they're on different sides doesn't mean we can't be friends.'

'No, of course not. But the thing is ... well, friends should be honest with each other. And what happened earlier, it made me think that maybe *we're* on different sides too — but I still want us to be friends.'

'How are we on different sides?' asked Jack.

'You wanted to report the gunmen, I'm on the side of the Volunteers.'

'I understand you being loyal to your dad, Emer. But that man threatened us.'

'I know. It was scary, and he shouldn't have done it. But apart from that, I believe in what the Volunteers stand for. It's not just loyalty to Dad.'

'And what do you think they stand for?'

'Irish independence. Or, at the very least, making the British give us Home Rule.'

'My da says lots of people don't want independence. And the Volunteers – he thinks that's going to lead to bloodshed and killing.'

'There's already bloodshed and killing,' answered Emer. 'The government is sending thousands of soldiers to die on the Western Front. Dad says one of the things the Volunteers stand for is making sure Irishmen aren't forced to fight in the British Army.'

'The government says there won't be conscription.'

'And they said the war would be over by last Christmas! Talk is cheap, Jack. But the Volunteers can stop the government if they try to force conscription.'

'That would be rebellion.'

'Well if *that's* rebellion, then it was rebellion when the loyalists formed a private army and started the Ulster Volunteer Force. But we didn't see the government disarming them.'

Jack looked like he was about to argue, but Emer continued, keeping her tone reasonable. 'Parliament passed the Home Rule Bill, and the UVF went out to block it by force. We need the Volunteers down here to stand up to that.'

'I'm not for the UVF, Emer. My da says there should be no private armies, north *or* south – and I agree.'

'So what do you want?' Emer watched as Jack breathed out, his sunlit face a study in concentration as he tried to marshal his thoughts.

'I want to be in the British Empire. And loads of people in Ireland do. I mean, we could have some sort of Home Rule and still be part of the Empire.'

'But why would you want to be?'

'Why *wouldn't* you?' countered Jack. 'Why turn your back on something so successful?'

'Successful for who, though?'

'The people who make up the Empire. Da says it's one of the most successful empires the world has ever known, and we're close to the heart of it. Why turn our backs on that prosperity?'

Emer looked at him questioningly. 'Prosperity? You've only to walk across Dublin to see hundreds of people who are hungry and dirt-poor.'

'I know, and that's all wrong. But we should be trying to make things fairer instead of rebelling against the government.'

'It's not rebelling if you take back your own country, Jack. Most of the English people I've met are really nice. But that's not the point. This is our country, not theirs. They fought us, took our land and occupied us.'

'That's history now.'

'And history can be changed. If we want to make history and

take back our country, we're entitled to. And if that means having to fight, so be it.'

Jack went quiet, and Emer hoped that they weren't going to fall out.

'We're not going to agree on this,' said Jack. 'Are we?'

'I suppose not. But I still want us to be friends.' Emer looked at him a little nervously. 'Do you?'

Jack nodded. 'Yes, definitely.'

Emer felt relieved. 'Well … maybe we should just agree to disagree then. All right?'

'Fair enough.'

'But I'm glad we talked about it, Jack. I felt it was kind of hanging between us, especially after this morning.'

'I know. You're better at this than me – I wouldn't have known how to bring it up.'

Emer grinned. 'Know what else I'm better at?'

'What?'

'Swimming. I'll give you an odd of five, then race you across the river to the fallen tree! One, two …'

Jack sprinted to the riverbank and jumped in. Emer was pleased that they had reached an understanding, and she finished counting, then ran to the bank and jumped into the river after her friend.

CHAPTER SIX

'Don't be silly, Jack,' said his mother as she parcelled up a sack of old clothes on the kitchen table. The air was warm with the bright summer sunshine flooding in the window.

'I'm not being silly, Ma. It's awkward giving someone I know my cast-off clothes.'

'You said yourself this boy lives in a shack, and his uncle hasn't a bean.'

'I know, but still ...'

'They'll be glad of it. Back-to-school time is expensive, so it's only right we help someone worse off than us.'

'I don't want to seem like we're being all high and mighty, Ma.'

'Lord save us, where do you get your notions? John, will you talk sense into this lad?' she said, addressing Jack's father, who was shaving at the kitchen sink.

Jack looked appealingly to his father, who wiped soap off his razor. Under the rules of the Dublin Metropolitan Police Da was obliged to shave every day – a ruling he took seriously – and now he carefully laid down his gleaming open razor and spoke to Jack.

'It does you credit, son, that you don't want to embarrass your friend.'

'He's not really a friend, Da, more a schoolmate.'

'Either way, your heart's in the right place. But Ma is being practical. With this lad and his uncle really poor, it's better they take some help rather than go without. All right?'

Da was usually reasonable, but once he put his foot down that was it – as Maureen had found out when she had to leave her Volunteer boyfriend. There had been an atmosphere for a while after that, but Ma and Da had stood firm, and Jack realised now that they were united on this issue too. 'OK,' he conceded, 'I'll bring Gerry the clothes.'

'Good lad,' said Ma.

'And here, get yourself a few nutty favours,' added Da, winking and slipping Jack a penny.

'Thanks, Da. Might as well do it now, I suppose,' he said, reaching out and taking up the sack of clothes. He bade farewell to his parents and made for the hall door. Stepping out into the sunshine, he decided it was too early to call for any of his friends, and instead he turned the corner into Ardmore Avenue and made for the steps that led down to Old Cabra Road. It was a nice morning for a walk to Gerry's cottage by the Tolka, and Jack decided that he would get the delivery of the parcel out of the way and then reward himself by buying sweets with Da's penny.

It was nice of Da to recognise his unease and give him the penny. Jack's mind went back to the previous week when his father had listened carefully while he gave a description of the gunman who had threatened him on the remote hillside. Da had been sympathetic and had praised Jack for his accurate depiction of the incident, saying he would be a good addition to the force when he was older.

Nothing further had come of the affair, however, and now Jack decided to put such thoughts from his mind and simply savour the warmth of the summer morning. Heading up the Old Cabra Road, he followed his usual route, crossing the sparkling waters of the Royal Canal at the lock near Broom Bridge, then descending into the valley where the Tolka glistened in the morning sunshine. Nobody was at the swimming hole this early in the day, and Jack walked past the gang's usual spot and up the trail towards Gerry's cottage. He had never been up to the building before, and as he drew near he saw that it was in a really bad state of repair. An ancient-looking cart lay in the yard to the side of the cottage, and a wild-eyed piebald horse grazed on nearby wasteland, tethered to a wooden stake. There was a faintly unpleasant animal smell in the air, and Jack lowered the sack, feeling nervous about knocking on the cottage door. Suddenly Gerry rounded the building, a bloodied rabbit carcass in his hands.

'Jack,' he said in surprise. 'What are you doing here?'

'I, eh … I came to see you. What are you doing with that?' asked Jack, indicating the bloodied remains of the rabbit.

'I'm just after guttin' it,' said Gerry easily. 'It'll be dinner for me and me uncle.'

'Right,' said Jack. He looked away from the carcass and told himself that it didn't make sense to be disgusted – their own meat was no doubt bloody when slaughtered by the local butcher. But he was still slightly shocked by Gerry's blood-stained hands.

'So what did you want me for?' asked Gerry, casually hanging the rabbit from a hook and wiping his hands on a filthy cloth.

'Eh … my ma thought you might get some use out of these,' said Jack, handing over the sack. 'It's clothes and shoes and stuff … you know … with the … with the school year coming up and all …' he said, knowing that he was blabbing due to his unease.

Gerry took the sack but said nothing, and Jack felt even more uncomfortable. *Why do my parents have to be such do-gooders,* he thought, *sticking their noses in where they aren't wanted?!*

After what felt like a long time, Gerry finally said 'thanks' and gave a curt nod.

Jack was relieved that the other boy had at least accepted the clothes, but he wasn't surprised that Gerry had been unenthusiastic. He might be poor, but he still had his pride. And in truth the two of them had never been friends, but rather classmates from very different backgrounds who nevertheless got on with each other. Gerry was regarded as a tough kid in school, and by being loosely associated with him Jack's standing was boosted. Not that Jack couldn't defend himself – his father had taught him to box. But Da had also insisted that he should always try to avoid fights, explaining that it would look bad for the son of a DMP man to get drawn into brawling. So being involved with Gerry had been handy. Now the other boy looked Jack in the eye, then reached into his pocket.

'Here, have an apple,' he said, and to Jack's surprise he pulled out a small but shiny red apple from his pocket.

'You don't have to,' said Jack.

'I want to.'

Jack realised that Gerry wasn't just being generous. He was also saving face, and Jack guessed that by giving something as well as taking something, he was striving to appear more like an equal.

'OK, then. Thanks, Gerry, it looks delicious,' he said, taking the apple and slipping it into his own pocket.

'I'll put these in and walk back to the river with you,' said Gerry, then he opened the door of the cottage and placed the sack of clothes inside.

Jack got a glimpse of the ragged-looking interior, but as Gerry went to leave, a harsh voice called out from within the cottage.

'Gerry?!'

'Yeah.'

'Get in here!'

The voice was slurred, and Jack suspected that Gerry's uncle might have been drinking.

'I was just going down to the river,' said Gerry. 'I'll be back in–'

'Get in here and don't argue with me!' shouted the unseen man. '*Now*, if you know what's good for you!'

Jack didn't want to get Gerry into trouble, so he spoke up quickly. 'Listen, I have to go anyway. I'll see you again.'

'OK, see you.'

As Jack started down the trail, he heard the sound of an angry, raised voice from inside the cottage. He hoped that Gerry would be OK and that his uncle wouldn't be violent with him. Jack had never seen his own father either drunk or violent. Struck by the contrast, he made his way down the hill, slightly ashamed of his earlier impatience with his parents and thinking that, when it came to families, he should probably count his blessings.

'It's like being in prison!' said Joan. 'I hate the first day back in school.'

'It's not all bad,' answered Emer. 'I like seeing the girls again.'

They were gathered in the classroom of their convent school, awaiting the arrival of their teacher, and the room was noisy with the excited chatter of pupils meeting up after the summer. Most of the time Emer enjoyed school, though she wished that Gladys could have been in her class, like Joan was. Gladys and her family were members of the Church of Ireland, however, so she went to a Protestant school, while Emer and Joan attended a Catholic convent school run by an order of nuns.

'Look on the bright side,' added Emer. 'We're going to have Miss Clarke again.'

'Yeah, I was praying we wouldn't get Sister Maureen,' replied Joan. She made a pious face and accurately mimicked the nun's northern accent. *'Every girl should have a favourite saint. Who are you devoted to, Joan Lawlor?'*

Emer laughed at her friend's impersonation. 'Well, Miss Clarke will never ask you that.'

'No,' said Joan. 'She'll just ask us what we think the stars are made of, or why women should have the vote, or what was the best song ever written!'

It was true that Miss Clarke was constantly encouraging them to think about all aspects of the world around them. She was a colourful Englishwoman in her thirties who had come to Ireland from the town of Hoylake, on the Wirral peninsula. Although she was a Catholic with Irish relations, she seemed exotic to her pupils, with her unpious attitude, her English accent and her wide-ranging enthusiasms.

'It's great that we'll have her for our last year in primary,' said Emer. 'I wasn't sure if we'd get her for two years in a row.'

'Yeah,' agreed Joan. 'We could have been landed with Miss Potter – with her bad breath and her big bum!'

Emer burst out laughing at her friend's cruel but accurate description, then she heard her name being called.

'Emer Davey!'

'Yes, Sister,' she answered, turning to find that Sister Assumpta, the vice principal, had silently entered the room.

'What have I said is inappropriate behaviour for a young lady?' asked the nun.

Emer swallowed nervously under the woman's gaze. Sister Assumpta was a disciplinarian who had the knack of arriving in a room soundlessly – hence her nickname, 'Creeper' – and many a pupil had regretted comments overheard by her. Emer tried to recall the most recent talk the nun had given before the summer break. 'Eh … girls shouldn't be heard whistling, Sister?'

'No, they should not. Nor should they be heard shouting or engaging in boisterous laughter – as you've just been.'

'Sorry, Sister.'

The vice principal was a small, thin woman, but what she lacked in size she made up for in authority, and now her piercing eyes bored into Emer. 'Perhaps you'd care to share the cause of your levity?'

Emer hesitated, and the nun continued impatiently. 'What were you laughing at?'

Emer knew that Joan would be in big trouble if she repeated her remark about Miss Potter, and she could see that her friend looked nervous. But she herself would be in even more trouble if Sister Assumpta caught her lying.

'Well?' said the nun.

'Just a joke, Sister,' answered Emer.

'Really? Kindly tell us what it was that provoked such unlady-like hilarity.'

Emer tried not to panic. She thought of Ben's joke about the swimming trunks, but the nun wouldn't approve. With her brain grasping desperately, she recalled a joke that Jack had told her. 'Why ... why is it easy to weigh fish?'

The nun indicated to continue.

'Because they have their own scales.'

It had seemed funny when Jack told it, but Sister Assumpta's dis-approving expression didn't change. Of course she wasn't interested in being amused by the joke, Emer thought – this was just punish-ment for laughing too loudly. Still, she had kept herself and Joan out of far bigger trouble by not revealing the Miss Potter remark.

Sister Assumpta kept her eyes locked on Emer's and spoke with quiet authority. 'No more guffawing. In future conduct yourself like a young lady.'

'Yes, Sister.'

Sister Assumpta turned around and pointed to a girl who was standing behind her. 'This is Catherine O'Flynn, girls. She joins us from St. Rita's.'

St. Rita's was a primary school in a nearby poorer area, and Emer picked up on the hint of distaste in Sister Assumpta's tone. Emer hated snobbery, though she knew it was widespread in Dublin – it even existed to a certain extent in her own family. Her mother had gone to a well-regarded convent school in Ennis, County Clare, and put great store in the privileges that her education had brought. Emer's father was more of a self-made man and had gone to a modest school in County Kildare before working his way up in the grocery trade. But Dad was class-conscious and happily paid the fees for Emer to be educated. Each year Emer's school allowed in several pupils who paid no fees, as a charitable gesture, and now Emer felt sorry for the new girl as she stood red-faced in front of the other pupils.

'Catherine will be joining us for sixth class, in an attempt to win a scholarship for secondary school,' continued Sister Assumpta.

Emer felt a stab of irritation. Why couldn't the vice principal have introduced her simply as a new pupil, without drawing attention to her background? Admittedly her poorer standing might have emerged in time, and maybe the nun wasn't being malicious, but Emer still felt that she had been insensitive.

'That will be all, girls,' said Sister Assumpta. 'Miss Clarke will be with you shortly. Meanwhile act with decorum.'

'Let's make the new girl feel welcome,' said Emer.

Joan looked hesitant. 'Lottie Brophy knows her already and says that she's not that friendly.'

'It doesn't matter. Creeper has embarrassed her. Let's show her that we're not all snobs.'

'OK.'

Emer started across the room, aware that Sister Assumpta had paused at the door and was watching her. Making a point of welcoming Catherine immediately after Sister Assumpta had criticised Emer for not being ladylike might annoy the nun, but she didn't care. She walked up to the new girl. 'Hello,' she said. 'I'm Emer and this is Joan. Welcome to sixth class.'

From the doorway she could see Sister Assumpta watching her, but she ignored the nun's stare, smiled at the newcomer, and reached out a welcoming hand.

'God, he looks like he's going to read the riot act!' said Ben as the captain of the swimming club stepped onto a podium in Tara Street Baths to address a gathering of club members.

'Look at his face,' whispered Joan. 'You'd think he'd swallowed a lemon!'

'Don't let him see you messing, Joan,' warned Gladys.

'Why? What'll he do, drown me in the pool?!'

Jack was amused by Joan's irreverence, but at the same time he didn't want to annoy the captain. Joan wasn't serious about swimming, but Jack was, especially now that he had mastered the art of breathing out into the water while doing the Australian crawl. He was still nowhere near Emer when it came to style and speed, but he had become a much better swimmer in the weeks since he had joined the club.

'Watch it, Joan,' whispered Ben now. 'He's looking at us!'

Jack watched as Joan adopted an innocent and attentive face, then the captain began to speak, and Jack gave him his full attention.

'I have details of the annual gala,' said the captain, a well-built man in his early forties who had a deep voice and a strong Dublin accent. 'It's going to be held this year on November the twelfth, in Iveagh Baths. So what are we going to do?'

'Swim in it?' whispered Ben, and Jack realised that Ben had been infected by Joan's giddiness. Jack wanted to laugh, but he kept his face serious as the captain looked down at the club members.

'We're going to win it!' said the captain. 'This is a chance for you all to prove yourselves. It's been seven years since we last won the cup, and it's high time we took it back. There'll be teams competing on every level, so I want to see you all training hard between now and November. OK?'

'OK!' answered the members, and Jack felt a tingle of excitement. *Maybe I could get on a team*, he thought to himself. He was at the bottom level, but he was making real progress, and the idea of swimming for the club sounded great.

The captain dismissed the members, and Jack followed his friends towards the exit. They passed the entrance to the public baths. Having lived all his life in a house with a bathroom, Jack had been surprised to find out that large numbers of Dubliners came to Tara Street Baths to wash themselves, paying here for soap and a towel. It shouldn't have surprised him really, considering that the city had seventy thousand people living in tenements – where fifty or sixty residents might share one toilet and have no bath – yet he had been taken aback to see poor people queuing up for their weekly wash.

Now Jack and his friends stepped out of the baths onto Tara Street. A hint of coolness in the air confirmed that summer had ended and autumn had arrived.

'I definitely want to get on the first team for the gala,' said Emer.

'Really?' said Joan. 'Sure it's just a load of races.'

'There's a big silver cup,' answered Emer. 'It's important.'

Jack thought it was typical of Joan to take nothing seriously. 'I'm with Emer,' he said. 'I think it would be brilliant to swim for the club.'

'Yes, but Emer's sure to get on a team,' said Gladys. 'The rest of us mightn't.'

'Well, you won't if you think like that,' said Ben to his sister. 'Our cricket coach says you always have to *think* you can win.'

'I'm just being realistic,' argued Gladys.

They turned onto Burgh Quay, making their way towards their tram stop, and Jack was distracted from the conversation by a newspaper billboard. It stated that the Germans had advanced one hundred and twenty miles since the Russian army had abandoned Warsaw. The recent news from the Gallipoli front was bad too, with reports of slaughter and disease, and horror stories of flies feeding off the countless corpses. Jack was worried for his uncle Bertie, who was caught up in the nightmare of Gallipoli, and also for his cousin Ronnie, who was enduring trench warfare in Belgium.

Jack's family rarely discussed their concerns about Bertie and Ronnie, as though by not mentioning the horror, they could keep it at bay. Jack sometimes talked about his fears to Ben, but Ben wasn't the sort of person who thought deeply about anything. Jack wished he could confide in Emer, who did think seriously about things, but that wasn't possible either. They had cleared the air about their families' opposing political views the day of the hike to Old Bawn. But it was one thing to agree to disagree, another to expect her to sympathise with his fears for his relations in the British Army.

'Penny for your thoughts, Jack!' said Emer now.

He smiled ruefully as he came out of his reverie. 'Just … just thinking that nothing is ever simple.'

'Well one thing is simple,' answered Emer. 'You'll have to train hard to get onto a team for the gala.'

'Yeah,' agreed Jack. 'And you know what – I'll make it!' His mind suddenly made up, he put aside his worries for now, then fell into step with his friends and headed for the tram stop.

CHAPTER SEVEN

'**G**ood news, boys!' said Brother McGill as he swept into the classroom. His flowing black robes caused the chalk dust suspended in the air to swirl, and it shimmered in the September sunshine that shone through the windows.

Jack felt relieved. Any break from the normal school routine was welcome, and Brother McGill could sometimes be distracted if asked the right kind of questions. They were about to have a class in algebra, a subject that Jack disliked, so he was pleased that the teacher had an announcement to make.

'The captain of the school's football team for this coming season has been decided upon,' said Brother McGill. 'And I'm very pleased to say that it's a boy from this class!'

Despite the teacher's good humour, Jack felt his heart sinking a little. It was going to be Phelim O'Connell, the boy he liked least in the class – he just knew it! Phelim was well-built and athletic and a skilful Gaelic footballer, but Jack had never got on well with him, and he didn't want the other boy's standing to be boosted by this honour. Phelim had been born in Connemara, so he spoke fluent Irish, which, along with his footballing ability, made him a favourite of Brother McGill's. He had a slightly nasty streak, however, and while he was too clever to bully anyone openly, he had a way of running down and excluding people he didn't like.

'It won't come as a huge surprise,' continued Brother McGill, 'when I tell you that the boy chosen as captain is none other than our own Phelim O'Connell!'

The rest of the pupils applauded. Jack reluctantly clapped too, knowing it would seem like defiance to the teacher if he didn't.

'*Go raibh maith agat*, Brother,' said Phelim, a pleased expression on his face as he thanked the teacher. 'I'll do my very best for the school. And maybe bring back the cup as well!'

'Good lad yourself,' said Brother McGill. 'I wouldn't doubt you!'

Jack looked across the aisle at Phelim's satisfied face and tried to hide his irritation. Normally pupils who toadied favour with the teachers were unpopular, but Phelim O'Connell was strong and admired as a footballer, so he got away with it.

'Right,' said Brother McGill good-humouredly, 'I know you're all dying to get going on quadratic equations, but first, the roll call.'

He began to call out the names of the pupils, with each boy answering in Irish with a cry of '*anseo*' to indicate his presence.

Jack had noticed that Gerry Quinn wasn't in school today. He recalled the demanding attitude of Gerry's uncle on the morning that he had brought the used clothes to the cottage, and he suspected that Gerry had been ordered to skip school to help his uncle with some job.

'Gerard Quinn,' called out Brother McGill now.

When there was no answer, Brother McGill looked up from the roll book. 'Quinn?'

'He's not in, Brother,' answered the boy who normally shared the desk with Gerry.

'Maybe he's taking his uncle's horse to the knackers' yard, Brother!' said Phelim.

Brother McGill smiled indulgently. Jack thought to himself that the teacher might have reacted differently if it hadn't been Phelim O'Connell who made the remark, or if the jibe had been about someone less poor than Gerry. Seeing that the brother hadn't disapproved, a lot of the boys laughed at Phelim's remark, but Jack didn't join in.

Jack knew that Gerry and his uncle collected waste food known as 'slops' from people's houses and sold it as swill to several of the city's piggeries. It was dirty, messy work, but someone had to do it, and Jack thought it was mean of Phelim to belittle their classmate because of what his uncle did.

Just then there was a knock on the classroom door, and a boy entered and approached Brother McGill. 'Sorry to disturb you, sir,' said the boy, 'but you're wanted in the teachers' room by Brother Quirke. He said it won't take long.'

Brother McGill rose from his desk. 'All right, boys, look over your equations and don't kick up a rumpus.'

As soon as the teacher left the classroom there was a buzz of conversation. Several of the boys congratulated Phelim O'Connell, and someone else asked what Gerry Quinn was doing, missing school on the first week back.

'Like I said, he might be bringing that nag to the knackers,' said

Phelim. 'Let's hope he has a good wash before he comes back into school!'

Some of the boys sitting nearby laughed, but Jack spoke up. 'You wouldn't say that to his face,' he said.

Phelim looked Jack in the eye, a hint of a smirk playing on his lips. 'Relax, Madigan, it was a joke.'

'It's not very funny. And you wouldn't say it if he was here.'

'Well, he's not here, so what he doesn't know won't hurt him. Unless of course you run telling tales.'

'I don't tell tales.'

'Then there's no problem,' said Phelim easily. 'He knows nothing, we've had a laugh, and you've sided with your down-and-out friend.'

'He's not a down-and-out,' said Jack. 'And if anyone in this class *was* down and out, you'd be the last person to help him.'

Jack saw a flash of anger in Phelim's eyes, but before he could react, the classroom door opened and Brother McGill re-entered. All the pupils hurriedly turned to their algebra books as though they had been studying. Jack and Phelim briefly locked eyes, however, and Jack sensed that they had just gone from not liking each other to being enemies.

'You forgot "The Universe",' said Emer, pointing to the cover of Joan's schoolbook. In bold block letters Joan had written her address as Ellesmere Avenue, North Circular Road, Dublin, Ireland, Europe, Northern Hemisphere, The World, The Milky Way.

'Brilliant!' said Joan, and Emer watched as her friend immediately added 'The Universe' to the address.

They were sitting at their desk for Miss Clarke's history class. Every Wednesday Miss Clarke allowed a slot where pupils could ask questions about any period in history, and it was Emer's favourite time in the school week. Today she felt slightly nervous, however, knowing that her question might be a little awkward for an Englishwoman like Miss Clarke.

'All right, girls, let us commence!' said the teacher, her slightly dramatic delivery and northern English accent reminding Emer how different she was to most of the other teachers.

'Question time,' said Miss Clarke. 'So, who has an incisive question to expand our horizons?!'

Emer raised her hand.

'Emer Davey. Pray proceed.'

'Why do people say England is a great democracy, Miss, when the king isn't elected by the people but just gets born into the job?'

Emer knew that lots of people regarded King George with awe and might find the question offensive. Miss Clarke was unconventional though, and Emer hoped that she wouldn't be annoyed.

The teacher raised an eyebrow. 'That's a challenging question. Is it prompted by your wish for Irish independence?'

Emer had made no secret in school of the fact that her family were nationalists, but she shook her head now. 'It's not just that, Miss. In countries like America and France they've no king, and the people elect their leaders. I wondered why the people in England don't want the same.'

Miss Clarke smiled wryly and nodded. 'It's actually a very good question. And there are people in England who don't want a monarchy. But are France and America as democratic as you make out?'

'Well, they vote for their presidents, don't they?' asked Emer.

'Yes, they do. But who does the voting? Not all the citizens. Certainly not the fifty percent of the population that's female.'

Emer already knew that Miss Clarke was in favour of the Suffragettes, who wanted votes for women. And Emer herself thought that votes for women was only fair, so she couldn't argue against that. 'I think every country should have votes for women, Miss,' she answered. 'But that doesn't change the fact that no-one elects the king. He just gets to rule by being born a prince.'

'Fair point,' conceded the teacher. 'Except that King George doesn't rule very much. The country is really run by Prime Minister Asquith and the Parliament, and the King is more of a figurehead.'

Emer enjoyed the way Miss Clarke treated you like an equal and argued intelligently, and now she tried to rally her own arguments. 'But even if he's a figurehead, Miss, how is it democracy if no-one has a say in picking him? And why should people who didn't choose him have to pay their taxes so he can have palaces and yachts?'

Miss Clarke shrugged. 'You can certainly make the case that

they shouldn't have to. If you want my personal view, I don't actually favour a monarchy. But here's the catch, Emer. Most people in Britain *want* a king. They *like* having a monarchy. So if most people want something, and they're getting what they want – is that not democracy too?'

Emer had never thought of it like that, and she didn't have a ready answer.

'You can say that every citizen should be equal,' continued Miss Clarke, 'and that you shouldn't have dukes looking down on earls, and earls looking down on barons, and all of them looking down on ordinary people. But with a king, there's an aristocracy, and most people in Britain aren't clamouring to be rid of that system. So it's a democracy, Emer, even if it's not the kind you and I might choose. All right?'

'Yes, Miss.'

'Good question though. And a good example of the fact that in history few things are black and white. The Romans were brutal conquerors, but they built wonderful roads and aqueducts. The Egyptians were great astronomers and mathematicians, yet they worshipped the sun and believed in slavery. History is full of contradictions, girls, and things are rarely all good or all bad – you'll usually find lots of grey areas. And if we're wise, we adjust to that.'

Miss Clarke looked around the class. 'Now, next question?'

'What was the Boston Tea Party all about, Miss?' asked one of the other girls, but Emer wasn't really paying attention as she tried to process what the teacher had said. Miss Clarke was certainly right about life being full of contradictions. Even in her own circle there was Jack, who was the son of a policeman and who believed in Ireland staying in the British Empire, yet who was a really good friend. And there was Catherine O'Flynn, the poorer girl whom Emer had welcomed to the class, but who, in the intervening weeks, had turned out to be ungrateful and a bit stand-offish. Even Sister Assumpta, whom Emer disliked as a snob and a stickler for all the petty rules, was also a highly dedicated teacher who put in many extra hours of tuition to ensure her pupils got the best possible education. And there was Miss Clarke herself: she had previously told the class that her father was a green-keeper at a golf course in Hoylake and that she had had to rely on a scholarship to go to teacher-training college, yet now she argued that Britain's class-conscious society was still democratic.

Emer tried to look interested in the Boston Tea Party, but her mind was racing. If everyone accepted all of life's contradictions and grey areas, how could anything ever be changed? And how could Ireland gain its freedom if there weren't people like her father, who didn't get bogged down in shades of grey but had a clear vision of independence?

Emer's train of thought was broken by a nudge from Joan. 'Well done,' she whispered. 'You gave Clarkie a run for her money!'

'Thanks, Joan,' she whispered back, then she sat up straight in the desk and tried to still her buzzing mind.

CHAPTER EIGHT

Jack surged through the water, kicking hard as he did a fast Australian crawl. Emer was leading the way in a race at the swimming hole on the Tolka, but Jack was ahead of Ben, Gladys and Joan as they navigated the improvised course. It involved crossing the narrow river several times and rounding a nearby rock in the water, and now Jack reached the finish in second place after Emer.

She was already out of the river, and she complimented him as he hoisted himself up onto the grassy bank. 'You're getting faster, Jack!'

'Thanks.'

'You have to be in with a good chance of making a team for the gala.'

Jack was pleased, knowing that Emer didn't pay false compliments. 'I really want to make it,' he admitted. 'I'll keep training hard.'

'Oh my God, I'm frozen to the marrow!' cried Joan as she hauled herself out of the water, followed by Ben and Gladys.

'Yeah,' said Ben, 'it's like the time our dad took a course of cold baths – pure torture!'

In the last week the temperature had dipped, and the friends had agreed that today would be the final river swim of the year. It was late September, and although they had enjoyed a lovely lingering summer, autumn had now definitely arrived. Even the Dublin Metropolitan Police hygiene rules had undergone their seasonal change. Members of the force were required to take two baths a week in summer and one bath a week the rest of the year. Jack's father prided himself on cleanliness and bathed more often than that, but it was still one of the milestones of the year for Jack when the DMP hygiene rules switched from summer to autumn.

His father had had a small cut over his eye at breakfast that morning. Da had made light of it – explaining that there had been a fracas in Kilmainham, where he served as part of the DMP's A Division – and Jack knew better than to press him for more information than he wanted to give. It reminded Jack of the dispute of two years previously, known as the Dublin Lock-out, when the police had frequently clashed with striking work-ers. Back then, Da had come home several times with cuts and bruises. Even though Jack looked up to his father and felt that he would never behave dishonourably, the Lockout had not been the DMP's finest hour, and there had been many claims of police brutality. Jack had had some sympathy for the striking workers, but his main concern had been for his father's safety. He hoped that last night's trouble in Kilmainham wasn't the beginning of more unrest.

'I'm not swimming in that river again till the sun is splitting the trees!' said Ben now as he and Jack towelled off and dressed behind a bush.

'Yes,' answered Jack, 'when your skin turns blue, it's time to stop swimming in the river!'

The girls had dried off and dressed behind a nearby bank of trees, and now all of them gathered on the riverbank. They sat on the bough of a fallen tree and sucked the Bullseye sweets that Emer had brought.

'Here's your friend,' said Joan, and Jack looked up to see Gerry Quinn approaching.

He gave his schoolmate a welcoming wave, and the others exchanged greetings with Gerry as he drew up beside them. Jack had never told Gerry about the argument with Phelim O'Connell, and Gerry had come to school the next day with a note excusing his absence. But the incident had made Jack feel closer to Gerry, and he was glad now when Emer offered him a Bullseye.

'Thanks,' said Gerry, popping it into his mouth, then indicating the river. 'Bleedin' freezin' for swimming.'

'Yes, much too cold,' answered Gladys, unable to disguise fully her disapproval of his language. 'This is our last swim of the year.'

'We should have a ceremony,' said Ben, 'like a farewell to the river.'

'Don't be daft, Ben,' said his sister.

'It's just marking the end of summer,' argued Ben, then he turned to Gerry. 'That's not daft, is it?'

Jack noted that Gerry looked surprised to be drawn into the discussion – he normally didn't get too involved with the group – but he shrugged, then replied, 'If you're a swimmer, I suppose it's no harm to mark the end of swimming.'

'Now,' said Ben, 'what did I tell you?'

'So how come you never swim, when you live beside the river?' asked Joan.

Gerry paused before answering. 'My uncle used to be a sailor. He said loads of sailors don't swim – that way they respect the water more. So he never taught me.'

'You could learn in our swimming club if you wanted,' said Ben.

'No,' said Gerry.

'Why not?' queried Joan.

'We couldn't afford it. And I'm not that bothered.'

'It's only three pence a week,' said Gladys.

'I haven't got three pence a week. Plus there'd be tram fares and all. I won't be doing it.'

Jack was used to Gerry's forthright manner, but he could see that the others were taken aback by his blunt admission of poverty. There was a slightly awkward pause, then Jack spoke up, wanting to make Gerry feel better. 'Well, I suppose being in a swimming club isn't the be-all and end-all.'

'That's rich coming from you!' cried Joan. 'You're trying like mad to make the team for this gala. You love the swimming club!'

Before Jack could respond, Gerry turned to Emer. 'Thanks for the sweet. See you around,' he added to the others, then started up the hill to his cottage.

Jack called out a farewell, then faced Joan. 'Why did you have to say that?'

'Say what?'

'That I love the swimming club. I was trying to play it down, so Gerry wouldn't feel bad.'

'It's not my fault if he's poor.'

'I didn't say it was. But it must be horrible having no money. We shouldn't do anything to make him feel worse.'

'There's loads of poor people in Dublin, Jack,' argued Joan. 'Are we supposed to worry about them all? Or apologise 'cause we can afford three pence a week for swimming and they can't?'

'I never said that.'

'But we're told to be charitable to the poor,' interjected Gladys. 'It says it in the bible.'

'It says lots of things in the bible,' answered Joan blithely.

'Maybe we should just change things,' said Emer. 'Maybe we should really change the country, so no-one is poor. Then nobody would need charity.'

Jack sensed that the conversation was going to get political, and he was relieved when Ben suddenly held up his hands.

'Enough arguing!' Ben cried. 'We came here to have the last swim of the year. So now it's time for the last picnic of the year. And I've got a whole slab of toffee cake. But anyone who wants a bit has to say "pretty please with a cherry on top"!'

The tension was broken, and Jack joined the others in having their picnic. But he couldn't help thinking of what Emer had said about really changing the country. If enough people shared her view, then there could be serious trouble ahead.

Emer stopped dead at the kitchen door when she saw her father holding the gun. The weapon was a Mauser pistol that had been part of a consignment smuggled into the country by the Irish Volunteers. Emer knew that her father was proud to be a captain in the Volunteers, and that he was pleased to be given the gun from the scarce supply of arms, but he didn't usually handle the Mauser in her presence.

'Emer,' he said, looking up in surprise, 'you're back early.'

'Miss Gildea is sick; the piano lesson was cancelled.'

'Ah,' said Dad, rising from the table and slipping the pistol into a drawer above the kitchen press. 'Nothing too serious, I hope?'

Emer realised that her father had been oiling the gun. She had known all along that the Volunteers were an army that might have to go to war, but she still felt a slight chill on seeing her father servicing a lethal weapon. Dad clearly didn't want to refer to the gun, however, so Emer followed his cue and instead answered his question. 'No, she just has a really bad head cold, so she put off the lesson.'

'Fair enough.'

'Dad, can I … can I ask you something?' said Emer, sitting at the kitchen table.

'Of course.' Her father looked at her encouragingly and sat beside her. 'What's buzzing round in that head of yours?'

'I was just thinking. If the Volunteers have their way, and we get independence … is it … is it definitely going to make things better for people?'

'How could it not? We'd be running our own affairs, instead of being ruled from England.'

'So poor people would get treated better?'

Her father looked at her enquiringly. 'What's brought this on, love?'

'There's a boy who goes to school with Jack. He's an orphan living with his uncle, and they're really poor, and his clothes are old, and his house is all run-down looking. And … well, he couldn't even afford three pence a week to be in the swimming club.'

'I'm sorry to hear that, pet.'

'So if Ireland gets her freedom, Dad, will it stop people having to live like that?'

Emer watched as her father breathed out. 'I'd love to tell you that it will, Emer. But I don't want to mislead you.'

'So … will it not?'

'Of course we'll change things. But we can't just wipe out poverty. It's like it says in the bible, "The poor you will always have with you".'

'But that was written two thousand years ago, Dad. Can we not make things better now? Especially if the British go, and we're starting from scratch.'

'There'll be lots of good things we'll do in a new Ireland. But life is never going to be the same for everybody. In any country there'll be people who work hard and succeed, and other people who don't.'

Emer knew that her parents' views were coloured by their own upbringings. Several members of Mam's family had held prized jobs in the postal service in County Clare – steady work that had provided the income to educate Mam, who in turn had been a postmistress before getting married. Dad had been apprenticed to the grocery trade, and by dint of very hard work had eventually managed to buy two shops of his own. But someone like Gerry Quinn was never going to get a start in the post office or the grocery trade, no matter how hard he might be prepared to work.

'I just think, Dad, that if you're going to … well, if you're going to risk your life fighting, it has to be worth it. To make a country where everyone has a fair chance.'

Her father looked at her seriously for a moment, then reached out and briefly stroked her hair with affection. 'I'm proud of you, Emer,' he said. 'I'm proud to have a daughter with such a good heart.'

Emer was touched, but before she could reply she heard the front door opening, and Mam came down the hall and into the kitchen.

'The budget's been announced!' she said dramatically.

'Well, tell us the worst,' said Dad.

Emer watched as her mother placed a newspaper down on the table, pointing to the front page. 'The government's put customs duty up fifty percent on tea and tobacco! And the halfpenny post is being abolished.'

Dad raised an eyebrow. 'Really? What about income tax?'

'Two and eleven pence halfpenny in the pound next tax year for anyone earning over one hundred and thirty pounds a year.'

'What?! That's a huge jump.'

'It's an absolute disgrace! We're paying through the nose so the British Army can spend millions of pounds waging war on Germany.'

It was unusual for her mother to get this agitated, and Emer listened as Mam continued her complaint. 'And the worst thing of all is that the Chancellor of the Exchequer had the cheek to say that he knows the taxpayer is determined to see the war through!'

'The sooner we make the break from Britain the better!' Dad said. 'This just confirms it.'

Emer hadn't been reassured by her father's response to her query about fairer conditions. She would have liked to question him a little more, but now was not the time. And so she said nothing while her father fumed about the budget, criticised the government as corrupt, and repeated his willingness to fight for independence.

CHAPTER NINE

The stinging smack of the leather made Jack wince as Brother McGill dished out the punishment. Even though he was in no danger of being beaten himself this time, Jack hated when other boys were slapped with the leather. It was a thick black strap specially made as an instrument of punishment, and rumour had it that there were copper coins sewn inside to make it heavier and therefore more painful for the victim.

Jack knew the paralysing pain that ran up your arm when you were slapped on the open palm by the leather, and he sympathised with Gerry Quinn, who was being beaten now.

Looking around the classroom, Jack could tell that there were boys who were happy enough to see Gerry being punished. He suspected that for some of them it was a sense of self-preservation, and a feeling that while the teacher's ire was focused on Gerry, it wasn't focused on them. For others, though, he reckoned that they enjoyed seeing another boy suffer, and Jack felt a familiar stab of distaste as he saw Phelim O'Connell watching the punishment with barely disguised relish.

'You won't mitch from school during my class, Mr Quinn!' cried Brother McGill as he brought the strap down on Gerry's hand, '*Seán Dubh* will teach you not to!'

Seán Dubh – Black John in Irish – was the nickname that Brother McGill had for his leather strap. Even though some of the boys laughed when the teacher jokingly referred to it this way, Jack never joined in, thinking that it was bad enough to be beaten without being expected to treat the cruelly designed leather as though it were somehow funny.

The teacher delivered two more hard slaps to Gerry's out-stretched hands. Jack couldn't help but admire the way Gerry bore the punishment, taking each stinging blow without crying out. Jack desperately wanted to tell Brother McGill to stop, that he was accusing Gerry in the wrong. Gerry had told Jack earlier that he hadn't actually been mitching from school at all, but had had to appear in court for trading with his uncle without a licence. Gerry's pride wouldn't let him tell the teacher that the family was up in court, so now he was taking a beating. Jack knew that he would be betraying a confidence if he told Brother McGill the truth, yet how long could he stay silent if the teacher continued beating an innocent boy?

Brother McGill unleashed two more blows, and Jack could see that Gerry was wracked with pain. *I can't let this continue*, he thought. *Even if Gerry hates me for telling, I have to stop it.* Dreading what he was about to do, Jack started to raise his hand to attract the teacher's attention.

'Let that be a lesson to ye all!' said Brother McGill, suddenly pocketing the leather and facing the pupils. 'Nobody mitches from my class – nobody!'

Jack quickly lowered his hand, then the bell rang to signal the end of the school day. Before Jack could sympathise with him, Gerry took his schoolbag and headed straight out the classroom door. Brother McGill gathered up his papers and left the room, and the boys relaxed. Jack sat unmoving in his desk.

The day had begun badly when his father had read in the newspaper that the army's latest Western Front offensive had met with varying success, with ground taken by the Allies in the morning sometimes quickly retaken by the enemy. Jack's cousin Ronnie was in a regiment reported to be in the thick of the fighting, and all of the family were really worried about him. Meanwhile the campaign in the Dardanelles had turned into a disaster, which meant that Uncle Bertie was a serious worry too. And now Gerry had just taken an unjustified beating.

'That eejit Quinn cost us an ecker-free night with his stupid mitching!' said the boy who shared a desk with Phelim O'Connell. This was a reference to Brother McGill's practice of letting the pupils off homework if all fifty-six boys in the class were in attendance and on time on a given day.

'He wasn't mitching,' said Jack.

'Then why did he take a hiding from Giller?'

'He had his reasons,' answered Jack, rising from his desk and taking up his schoolbag.

'What reasons?' asked Phelim O'Connell.

'You don't need to know them. But he wasn't mitching.'

Phelim looked at Jack with a sneer. 'You've become his little buddy, haven't you? Do you collect rags and bones together?'

Jack would have liked to wipe the smirk from Phelim's face, but he kept his temper and gave him a contemptuous look, then made to move off.

'I asked you a question,' said Phelim, gripping Jack's arm to stop him from leaving.

'Get your hand off my arm.'

Phelim looked at him challengingly. 'Or?'

Phelim was well-built and athletic, but Jack figured that a quick uppercut would leave him reeling. He balled his fist, then hesitated. He remembered Da's instruction when he had taught him boxing for self-defence: *You're a policeman's son, Jack. You can't be brawling. Always walk away when you can.*

Jack looked Phelim in the eye, struggling hard against the temptation to punch away his smirk. Without warning Jack pushed him hard with his left hand, simultaneously freeing his right hand. Phelim was taken by surprise and stumbled back a little, and Jack immediately hoisted his schoolbag and walked briskly to the classroom door.

'That's right, Madigan, run away,' called Phelim as Jack reached the door.

Even though Jack knew that he had done the right thing in obeying his father, it still felt wrong to walk off. He paused at the door, Phelim's taunt ringing in his ears. Then he took a deep breath, opened the door and walked out of the classroom.

'Don't say a word to Jack about any of this,' said Emer's father, indicating his packed kitbag on the breakfast table. 'We don't want Sergeant Madigan reporting it to his superiors.'

'I wouldn't,' Emer answered, knowing that Dad was going out on a day's armed manoeuvres with the Irish Volunteers. 'But Jack's no informer.'

'Jack is a grand lad, and I know he's your friend. But the Madigans are on the other side, Emer. Never forget that. Especially if things come to a head.'

It was a disturbing thought, and even now, several hours after that conversation with her father, it was still casting a slight shadow over Emer's day. She had arranged to go blackberry picking with the rest of the gang, and they had set off in the hazy October sunshine. They carried metal cans and hooked sticks for pulling down the high branches of the blackberry bushes that grew along the banks of the Royal Canal. Despite her father's warning Emer tried to behave normally with Jack, but of course she said nothing about the manoeuvres. She thought it was a pity, though, to have to be on guard with a friend, and wished life wasn't so complicated.

'Oh, by the way, we've bad news,' said Ben as they left behind the Old Cabra Road and made for the canal.

'Yeah?' said Emer.

Gladys looked uncomfortable. 'Don't be annoyed with us, Emer, but we're going to have to skip the gala.'

'Really?'

'I mean, we mightn't have made it onto a team anyway, but we won't even be able to cheer you on,' said Ben.

'Why not?'

'Our Sunday School choir is singing in a festival,' answered Gladys with an apologetic grimace. 'We just found out that it clashes with the gala. Sorry, Emer.'

'You'll really miss out!' said Joan. 'I heard that after the gala the captain treats everyone to fish and chips.'

'There's nothing we can do,' said Gladys. 'The vicar only told us at Sunday School today that he's changed our slot.'

Emer felt like protesting, but she didn't. She was a Catholic, as were Jack and Joan, whereas Ben and Gladys were Protestants. Despite her disappointment, she felt that she couldn't criticise the Protestant vicar. It was another complication in life that Emer wished she hadn't got to deal with, but her parents had taught her to be polite when dealing with other people's faiths. It was a relief then when Ben himself went on the attack.

'I liked the old vicar,' he said, 'but this new fella, he's really a pain.'

'How's that?' asked Jack.

'Always going on about sin – and alcohol. He's dead set against alcohol.'

'I'll drink to that!' said Joan, raising an imaginary glass.

The others laughed, though Emer knew that alcohol had become a major topic since the start of the war. Drinking was said to affect factory output for the war effort, and David Lloyd George, the politician, had claimed that the enemy consisted of

'Germany, Austria and drink'! Emer's parents drank in moderation, but her father had laughed at the new rule making it illegal for workers to buy rounds of drink in the pub.

Swinging their berry cans as they walked, the friends reached the canal lock. Emer breathed in, savouring the autumn scents of burning leaves and ripe fruit, and the canal's distinctive reedy smell. They crossed the railway track and the canal, then climbed over a gate into a nearby field to get access to the rear side of the towpath's blackberry bushes. They knew the fruit there wouldn't have been taken already by casual strollers.

'OK, anyone who doesn't fill their bucket is a hairy ape!' cried Joan.

They all began to pick fruit. Joan had borrowed her walking stick from her granny, and now she used it to hook the higher branches, where the most luscious berries seemed to grow. After an initial flurry the gang settled into a relaxed rhythm as it became obvious that there was no need to race, and that there were plenty of berries for everyone. Emer liked the sound of the berries hitting the bottom of the tin and the taste of the fruit as she occasionally popped a blackberry into her mouth with purple-stained fingers.

After a few moments she found herself working alongside Jack, and she indicated the direction of the fields leading down to the Tolka. 'We could call down for Gerry, if you like.'

Jack immediately shook his head. 'No, I think it's best to leave Gerry be.'

Emer was immediately curious. 'Really? What's wrong?'

Jack hesitated, then lowered his can and looked directly at Emer. 'If I tell you a secret, will you keep it to yourself?'

'Of course.'

'Da doesn't normally tell me police business,' said Jack quietly, 'but … well, he told me that Gerry's uncle has been charged with selling *poitín*.'

Emer knew that this was a strong alcoholic drink that was brewed and sold illicitly. 'Gosh. Could he go to prison?'

'He could. But he probably won't. Da thinks he should get off with a fine. But Da told me not to go anywhere near their house.'

'Right. And does Gerry know that you know?'

'No. It's a secret from him as well. But please, don't say anything to the others.'

'I can keep a secret, Jack.'

'I know you can,' he said, then he nodded and went back to picking blackberries.

Emer's mind started to race. Was Jack hinting that he knew she was keeping quiet about her father? And that maybe Mr Madigan knew about things like the Mauser, and the manoeuvres, and other illegal activities involving the Volunteers? Surely not. But she wasn't certain. Whatever the situation, she couldn't possibly ask Jack. And so she slowly breathed out, went back to picking the blackberries and wished, yet again, that life could be simpler.

CHAPTER TEN

Jack saw from his mother's face that something was badly wrong. He had been doing his homework at the kitchen table when there was a knock on the front door. Da was sitting at the fire reading the newspaper, Mary and Una were drinking tea and gossiping about other workers in the munitions factory, Maureen was out at the cinema, and Sheila and Ma had been working together, making a fancy hat.

'What is it, Helen?' said Da now, taking in Ma's expression as she returned from the hall.

In answer Ma raised her hand, showing a buff envelope. 'Telegram,' she said, a quiver in her voice.

Jack felt his pulses quickening. Thousands of Irishmen were fighting in the British Army, and their families dreaded the arrival of telegrams. The government notified the next of kin when soldiers were killed in battle, and already families all over Ireland had been devastated by the delivery of the kind of envelope that Ma now held.

'I ... I can't bear to open it,' she said, and Jack felt a surge of sympathy for her. Uncle Bertie was her brother, and Ma would be heartbroken if he had been killed. But Bertie was married, so surely his own wife would get the telegram if the worst had happened?

Before Jack could think about it any further, Da stood up.

'Do you want me to open it?' he asked gently.

Mary and Una were sitting as though transfixed, their tea cups on the table before them. Sheila had lowered the hat, her face white.

Ma didn't answer, just nodded instead as she handed Da the telegram.

Jack noticed that his father's hands were trembling slightly as he opened the envelope. Da took out the telegram, quickly read it, and turned to Ma.

'It's not Bertie. Josie sent this from Manchester. Ronnie … Ronnie was badly injured during shelling. He's in a hospital near Loos and he's … he's lost a leg.'

'Oh God, no!' cried Ma. 'No …'

'I'm sorry, Helen,' said Da.

But Ma was already in tears. 'Poor Ronnie, he's … he's a lovely lad. And now …'

Da reached out and squeezed Ma's arm. Jack couldn't bear to see the sorrow on her face. He thought of his cousin, who had been a talented soccer player, and he swallowed hard, trying to stop the tears welling up in his own eyes.

'At least he wasn't killed, Ma,' said Mary.

'Yeah, and he'll be out of the war now,' added Una.

Jack could see that his sisters meant well in trying to console Ma. But weren't the shells that Mary and Una made in their factory just like the shell that had taken his cousin's leg?

'He'll be crippled for the rest of his life,' said Ma with a sob.

'Why don't you sit down, Ma, and I'll make a fresh pot of tea,' suggested Sheila.

'I don't want tea!' she answered. 'Sorry, pet, I don't mean to snap at you, it's just ...'

'It's all right, Ma,' said Sheila softly. 'It's all right.'

'And at least Bertie is out of Gallipoli,' added Da. 'He'll be better off in Greece.'

Jack had heard that his uncle's unit had been evacuated from the horrors of Gallipoli and was now in Salonika.

'I wanted them both back safely,' said Ma, 'but now ...'

The tears ran down his mother's face, and Jack surreptitiously wiped his own eyes dry.

'I ... I'm going to go up and lie down for a bit,' said Ma.

'Will I come up with you?' asked Da.

'No, I just ... I just need to be on my own for a bit, John. I'll be fine, but I want to lie down.'

'Whatever you want, love,' said Da, and Jack sensed that his father felt as helpless as the rest of the family when it came to consoling Ma. She quickly squeezed Da's hand, then left the kitchen and made for her room. Jack listened as she ascended the stairs, then he heard the door of his parents' bedroom closing overhead.

'I know it's awful about Ronnie's leg,' said Mary, 'but isn't it better to have one leg and still be alive?'

'That's easy for you to say,' answered Jack, irritated by his sister's slightly breezy tone.

'I'm just saying. You don't have to bite my head off!'

'Please,' said Da. 'No arguing. Not tonight.' He placed one hand on Jack's shoulder and one hand on Mary's arm. 'Tonight let's just pull together as a family, OK?'

'Yeah. Sorry, Da,' said Jack.

'I'm sorry too,' said Mary. 'I didn't mean to ... to make light of what happened Ronnie.'

'I know,' answered Da, sitting with them at the table.

'What you said about Uncle Bertie, Da?' asked Jack.

'Yeah?'

'How safe is he in Salonika?'

'Nowhere's really safe, but it's better than fighting the Turks in Gallipoli.'

'I find it really confusing,' said Sheila. 'Why was he sent to Salonika?'

'To take on the Bulgarians.'

'The Bulgarians? What have they got against us?'

Da shrugged tiredly. 'They haven't anything against us, Sheila – no more than we have against them. But war takes on a life of its own. It spreads and spreads, and other countries get sucked in. Why don't you make that fresh pot of tea now? I think we could all do with a cuppa.'

Jack watched as his sister put on the kettle, his thoughts on what Da had said about war. He was hugely relieved that Da wasn't fighting in Loos or Gallipoli, but supposing the Irish Volunteers went to war here in Dublin? The DMP was an unarmed force, but they could quickly become involved in the conflict, just like numerous countries had been drawn into the war. Jack couldn't bear the thought of anything happening to Da, and so he said a quick prayer for his father's safety, then reluctantly went back to his homework.

'They said we couldn't do it, girls, and they were wrong!' said Miss Clarke.

Emer loved when her teacher departed from normal lessons to comment on the news of the day, and this afternoon she was in full flow about women replacing male workers who were fighting in the war.

'All those tasks that they said were "men's jobs" – now women are doing them, and often doing them better!'

Emer was fascinated by Miss Clarke's views. She realised from listening to her that the British ruling class didn't keep just the Irish in their place but also working-class English people, especially women. Miss Clarke had regaled her pupils with stories about the men-only golf club where her father worked as a green-keeper, where women in the clubhouse were usually either serving food or cleaning the premises.

'Now we're showing the powers-that-be there's nothing we can't do,' said the teacher. 'Only today the government announced that women can apply to be conductors on buses and trams.'

'I don't think I'd fancy working on a tram, Miss,' said Joan.

'Perhaps not,' said Miss Clarke. 'But isn't that the point, Joan? Now you have a *choice*. Now you can say "yes, I'd like that" or "no, I wouldn't like that". Personal freedom is about having choices.'

Just then the classroom door opened, and Sister Assumpta entered to take the class in religious instruction.

'Ah, Sister,' said Miss Clarke.

'Please finish whatever you're at, Miss Clarke. I'm probably a trifle early.'

Emer had noted that the two women were always polite to each other, but she got the feeling that there wasn't much warmth between them. Sister Assumpta was conservative about everything, whereas Miss Clarke was more progressive. But while the English-woman could sometimes be a little irreverent with the girls, she was a dedicated teacher and a Catholic, and Emer suspected that she was smart enough never to give Sister Assumpta anything with which to reprimand her.

'Just telling the girls about the decision to allow women conductors on buses and trams,' Miss Clarke said to the nun before turning back to the class. 'Very well, girls, your homework tonight is the essay we discussed, "A Day in the Countryside".'

Miss Clarke left the room, and Sister Assumpta moved behind the teacher's desk.

'Conductors on trams and buses – really!'

The scholarship girl, Catherine O'Flynn, was the daughter of a bus conductor, and Emer thought it would be horrible for

Catherine if Sister Assumpta belittled the role. Even though Emer didn't find the other girl very friendly, she didn't want to see her embarrassed in front of the whole class. She quickly raised her hand to try to get the nun's attention, but Sister Assumpta continued speaking. 'I hardly think any young lady would seek such a demeaning, masculine job. Who would wish to be a bus conductor?'

Catherine O'Flynn looked uncomfortable. 'My … my father is a bus conductor, Sister,' she said.

'Yes. So well he might be,' said the nun briskly, then she turned to Emer. 'Emer Davey, you had your hand raised.'

Emer felt a stab of panic, not knowing how to respond. She was going to ask Sister Assumpta for a word in private, to let her know that Catherine's father was a bus conductor. But now the damage was done, and Catherine looked humiliated.

'What was it you wanted?' said the nun.

'Eh … could we speak in private, Sister?' said Emer haltingly as she tried to work out how to handle this.

'Very well, approach the desk.'

Emer rose and walked up towards the teacher's desk. Sister Assumpta stepped into the corner of the room furthest from the class and indicated for Emer to join her there.

'Go over your catechism, girls. I'll be asking questions about the sacrament of Baptism,' Sister Assumpta said to the class, then she turned to Emer. 'Well?'

'It's … it's actually too late now, Sister,' said Emer in a low voice. 'I was just trying to save embarrassment.'

'Really?'

'I knew that Catherine O'Flynn's father is a bus conductor.'

'It can't be helped if she's embarrassed by her father's job.'

'No, I meant saving *you* embarrassment, Sister.'

'Saving *me* embarrassment?'

'I wanted to tip you off – so you wouldn't show her up. Remember you told us that good manners means never making other people uncomfortable?'

Sister Assumpta flushed slightly, then she looked accusingly at Emer. 'Are you presuming to teach me manners?'

'No, Sister. I just thought you wouldn't want … well, to put your foot in it.'

'Don't you dare lecture me on my behaviour!'

Emer said nothing, and the nun looked at her challengingly. 'Is that clear?'

'Yes, Sister.'

There was another pause. Emer felt that, despite her irritation, Sister Assumpta had been put on the back foot a little.

'Go back to your place now,' the nun finally replied. 'And watch your own behaviour.'

'Yes, Sister,' said Emer, then she made her way back to her desk, careful not to let any satisfaction show, but pleased to have made her point.

Jack hated the way Brother McGill made Phelim O'Connell the pet of the class. Even allowing for the teacher's love of everything Gaelic, Jack felt that he should be more even-handed with his pupils. But Phelim spoke fluent Irish and was captain of the school's Gaelic football team, so Giller indulged him.

Brother McGill looked approvingly at Phelim now as he raised his hand. 'Phelim?'

'Is it true, Brother, that the Germans are winning the war in Serbia hands down?'

The teacher nodded happily. 'It is indeed. The Germans and the Austrians are said to be in full control. So that's one in the eye for John Bull and the British Empire!'

Jack felt his anger rising. He expected Phelim to take pleasure in German victories, but Brother McGill must surely have known that there were several boys in the class with relations fighting in the British Army.

It was only two days since Jack had heard the awful news about his cousin Ronnie, and the memory was still raw. Ma had gotten over the initial shock of her nephew losing his leg, but the family was still really saddened. Jack felt outraged by Brother McGill's flippant take on a war that had so far cost half a million British casualties.

The bell sounded for the end of the school day, and Jack felt both relieved and frustrated. He hated the teacher's attitude, yet to challenge someone of Brother McGill's authority was almost unthinkable. The teacher gathered up his books and left the classroom, and Jack breathed deeply, trying to calm himself.

He could understand people being against the idea of the British Empire, but to be disrespectful of the thousands of soldiers who had died was horrible. Still, there was nothing he could do now, so he began to pack his copybooks into his schoolbag. A shadow fell across his desk, and Jack looked up to see Phelim standing before him. It was a month now since Jack had pushed him away and walked off to avoid a fight, but there was still simmering bad blood between them.

'So what do you think, Madigan?' said Phelim with a smirk. 'First Gallipoli and now Serbia – seems like your precious Allies are getting their backsides kicked.'

'They're not losing on the Western Front,' said Jack. 'And that's where the main war's being fought.'

'Oh yeah, the Western Front. They're doing great there. Hiding in trenches and living like rats!'

'You don't know what you're talking about!'

'Don't I?'

'They're not hiding,' said Jack, 'they're fighting really bravely.'

'How do you know if they're brave? Half of them could be cowards.'

'They're not cowards! My cousin Ronnie lost his leg fighting there!'

Phelim raised an eyebrow in surprise. 'Lost his leg?'

'Yeah.'

'That was a bit careless. Has he found it yet?'

Jack shot out from the desk and swung his fist at the other boy, but Phelim had pulled back out of range. Jack immediately went after him, but found his way blocked by Gerry Quinn.

'Leave it, Jack, he's not worth it,' said Gerry, firmly holding him back.

'Yeah, leave it, Jack, if you know what's good for you,' said Phelim. 'I don't want to have to burst your face.'

Still holding Jack back, Gerry turned to Phelim. 'You won't be bursting anyone's face, O'Connell. Though if you want your go, you could try and burst mine.'

'Really?' said Phelim.

'Yeah, really.'

Phelim smirked and looked at Jack. 'Just as well you have someone to hide behind, Madigan.'

Before Jack could reply, Gerry turned and whispered to him, 'Let me handle him.'

Jack knew that Gerry was an experienced street fighter, and he was grateful for his support. But he would lose face if he let the other boy fight for him, and besides, he was really angry with Phelim for insulting his wounded cousin, and he wanted to do this himself. He thought briefly of Da's rule about walking away where possible, but decided it wasn't possible this time. 'Thanks, Gerry,' he said, 'but it's OK.'

He turned to Phelim and spoke with quiet fury. 'Outside, O'Connell, at the back of the handball alley.'

'Your funeral,' said Phelim.

'We'll see about that,' said Jack, grabbing his schoolbag and striding for the door, then going down the corridor and out into the yard.

'Mill! Mill, at the handball alley!' he heard boys calling out behind him in the schoolyard.

A moment later he rounded the corner, past the high wall of the alley. The rest of the class quickly followed him, and in spite of the chill autumn breeze Jack took off his sweater and handed it with his schoolbag to Gerry. Phelim stripped off his sweater also and gave it to one of his friends.

'OK, Madigan. Let's see what you're made of!' he said.

Jack still felt angry, but he knew that to win he had to control his anger and think tactically. Phelim was bigger and heavier than him, yet Jack had some advantages. Phelim didn't know that he had been taught how to box. And because Jack hadn't used his fists before and wasn't regarded as a fighter, Phelim was over-confident. The key to winning would be to strike hard early on, before Phelim realised what he was up against. But even if it turned into a dog-fight and he got hurt, then so be it – he couldn't let the other boy away with belittling Ronnie.

Jack raised his fists as Phelim advanced, but he didn't adopt the traditional boxer's stance, wanting to keep his boxing training a surprise until the last minute. Phelim suddenly rushed at him, launching a punch towards Jack's face. Jack danced sideways, dodging the blow and landing a right-hand jab into Phelim's ribs as the other boy's momentum carried him past. The blow obviously hurt, and Phelim cried out in anger, then wheeled around and made for Jack again. Once again Jack kept his guard low, but when Phelim swung a punch at his jaw, he quickly shot up his left hand and blocked the blow, as Da had taught him. Jack immediately bounced forward and drove his fist hard into Phelim's solar plexus, and the bigger boy doubled up in pain. As his opponent gasped for air, Jack unleashed a blow to his ribs followed by a stinging right hook that split Phelim's lip and sent him staggering to the ground.

There was an animal-like roar from the watching boys. Jack looked at his dazed opponent crouched on the ground with blood pouring from his lip. Part of him was sickened by what he had done, but part of him was exhilarated too, and he drew nearer to Phelim. 'That's for insulting my cousin and calling brave men cowards!' he said.

He turned away and took his sweater and schoolbag from Gerry, then he walked off, his exhilaration quickly fading as he thought of the consequences of what he had done.

CHAPTER ELEVEN

'I know the killer!' said Joan. 'It's definitely the fella with the squinty eye!'

'Too obvious,' said Emer as she walked home along the North Circular Road with Joan, Jack, Ben and Gladys. They had been to the moving pictures in the Bohemian Cinema in Phibsboro to see the first instalment in a two–part mystery drama.

Emer loved their Sunday afternoon trips to the cinema. The Bohemian had its own distinctive smell, and she liked the magic of the flickering images in the darkened auditorium and the improvised piano music played live by an accompanist as the story unfolded.

'I still say it's the squinty fella,' said Joan. 'He looks like he'd kill you!'

'But we shouldn't judge people by their looks,' said Gladys. 'Mr Prendergast always says that.'

'Who's Mr Prendergast when he's at home?' asked Joan.

'Our Sunday School teacher,' answered Ben. 'But he also thinks that people shouldn't play cricket on a Sunday, so you have to take him with a grain of salt!'

'Who do you think is the killer, Jack?' asked Emer, aware that her friend was a bit subdued.

'I'd say it's the sister. You're always worried that the killer will murder her – so it'd be a really good twist if she's the killer herself.'

'I'd never have thought of that,' said Gladys.

'Yeah, but it makes sense,' said Ben. 'Good thinking, Jack.'

'Thanks.'

They paused at the railway bridge, and the crisp air of late October suddenly filled with black smoke as a locomotive from the Midland Great Western Railway chugged beneath them, heading north towards Liffey Junction. They waited until the train passed, the pungent smoke still swirling about, then Emer made a point of falling into step with Jack behind the others as they started for home again.

Jack had told her about his fight a couple of days previously and his concerns about what might happen when he arrived in school tomorrow morning. Even though she couldn't root for the British Army the way Jack did, Emer still felt that the boy Jack had fought was horrible to say what he had, and that he had deserved it when Jack defeated him.

'Are you still worried about the fight?' she asked now.

Jack nodded. 'I don't know whether I should have told my da or not.'

'By telling, you might give him worries he doesn't need. If you say nothing, it could all blow over.'

Jack looked at her appealingly. 'Do you really think it'll blow over?'

'Lots of boys have fights and don't tell their parents. Maybe they should, but a lot of them don't. And seeing as this Phelim lost, he probably won't want to draw attention to it.'

'Yeah, you could be right,' said Jack more hopefully.

Emer was glad that she had cheered her friend up a little, and she turned to him and smiled. 'And talking of fighting, did you hear about the boxer who was offered a fight for the crown?'

'No.'

'He said: "Great, I think I can beat the Queen in about three rounds!"'

Jack laughed, and Emer was pleased. She liked the way his eyes sparkled when he laughed, and she thought he looked far more like himself when he was happy. She hoped that the advice she had given him was good and that he wouldn't get into trouble. Then she said a prayer under her breath, crossed her fingers for luck and carried on for home.

Al Jolson sang 'Sister Susie's Sewing Shirts for Soldiers' on the gramophone in the living room, but Jack didn't join in tonight. Since Mary and Una had begun working in the munitions factory, they had money to spare, and normally Jack loved singing along to the gramophone records on which they spent much of their wages. Now, though, he felt his knees trembling as he left his sisters and mother behind and stepped out into the hall. He paused before the parlour door, dreading facing Da yet knowing that putting it off was just prolonging his agony.

His father had been called to the school by Brother McGill today. Although Jack didn't blame Emer, he wished that he hadn't followed her advice in not telling Da about the fight. But it had been his choice, and now he had to face Da and take whatever punishment came his way. He swallowed hard, then knocked on the parlour door and entered. Da was sitting up very straight in his chair, and Jack knew from his tight lips and the look in his eyes that he was angry.

'Close the door and sit down, Jack,' he said.

Jack did as he was told, and his father looked at him a moment then breathed out.

'Obviously you know what this is about.'

'Yes.'

'None of our other children ever caused Ma or me to be summoned to the school. Yet here I was today, having to leave work early to meet Brother McGill.'

'I'm sorry, Da, I–'

'Don't interrupt me! You'll have the chance to say your piece, but for now you hold your tongue.'

'Yes, Da.'

'We had a conversation some time back about integrity. How not saying anything can have the same effect as telling a lie. Do you remember?'

'Yes, Da.'

'Yet you kept all of this from me. You got into a brawl, you injured a boy who captains the Gaelic team. Because of his injury his parents stopped him from playing in a match last weekend – a match the school narrowly lost in his absence. His parents are upset, Brother McGill is upset, but most of all Ma and I are disappointed. You're going to have to be punished for this, Jack.'

Jack felt his mouth going dry, but he swallowed and looked appealingly at his father. 'Can I … can I tell you my side of it?'

Da nodded. 'You can. But by God, it better be good.'

'It's … it's not completely good, Da,' admitted Jack. 'But I didn't tell you because I thought it might all blow over, and that Phelim O'Connell would just take his beating. I really didn't want to worry you for no reason. On my word of honour, Da, that's part of why I said nothing.'

His father looked at him, then nodded. 'Maybe so, but that doesn't change the fact that you split this boy's lip so badly he couldn't play for the school.'

'I'm sorry it affected the school, Da. Really, I am. But … well, fighting Phelim O'Connell shouldn't be different to fighting any other boy. Just 'cause he's good at football shouldn't make him special, shouldn't make him matter more than other boys.'

Even though Da was clearly angry, Jack knew that he prided himself on being fair, and that as a policeman he always listened to evidence from both sides of any dispute. His father said nothing now, but Jack suspected that his point had been noted.

'As for the boxing, Da, I only hit him two or three times. I could have hurt him a lot more and I didn't.'

'That was big of you,' said Da sarcastically. 'But I seem to remember teaching you boxing for self-defence. Is that how you remember it?'

'Yes, Da.'

'But this wasn't self-defence. This was an arranged fight behind the handball alley. Or is that untrue? Has Brother McGill been misleading me also?'

'No. But—'

'But? Another but?'

'It's true what Brother McGill said, but there's more to it than that,' said Jack.

'Let's hear it then.'

'Well … did … did Brother McGill say what the fight was about?' asked Jack.

'No. It was enough for him that you injured another boy.'

'But you're fairer than him, Da. Surely it matters to you *why* it happened?'

His father looked thoughtful, then nodded. 'Go on then, why did it happen?'

'Phelim O'Connell insulted Uncle Bertie and our cousin Ronnie. He's dead against the British Army. He said that the soldiers on the front were cowards, and when I said that Ronnie had lost his leg, he made a joke of it.'

'Yeah?'

'I saw red, Da. I'm sorry, I know I've let you down. But I couldn't bear to hear him calling brave men cowards and making fun of Ronnie after what he's been through.'

Jack looked at his father and saw that his expression had changed.

'This Phelim O'Connell … He sounds like an ill-mannered pup.'

'He's not nice, Da,' said Jack, his hopes rising that maybe Da wouldn't punish him too much now that he had explained.

'And he really made fun of Ronnie? Even though he knew he'd lost his leg?'

Jack nodded. 'He said that was careless, and could he not find the leg again?'

Jack saw a flash of anger in his father's eyes.

Da said nothing for a moment, then sighed. 'This changes the complexion of things,' he said. 'Not that I approve of brawling, mind – it still reflects badly on me as a policeman.'

'I know, Da, and I'm really sorry.'

'Having said that, it sounds like this O'Connell pup needs manners put on him.'

Jack held his breath, hardly daring to think that his father had been swayed.

Da stroked his chin, then looked at Jack. 'I still have to punish you. I told Brother McGill that I would.'

'Really?'

'So for the next two weeks, I'm docking your pocket money by two pence.'

Jack could hardly believe his luck.

Da continued, his tone severe. 'This punishment won't be discussed with any others. *Anyone at all*, you understand?'

'Yes, Da.'

'So I'll write and inform Brother McGill that you're being punished, you will be punished, and that will be the end of the matter.'

Jack felt like cheering, but he knew not to show that his father was practically letting him off.

'OK, Da, I understand,' he said.

'But next time something happens, Jack, don't keep it from me.'

'I won't.'

'Right then, that will be all.'

'OK, Da,' said Jack, rising to his feet.

'And Jack?'

'Yes, Da?'

His father paused, as though seeking the right words. 'You're a good lad. Go on now.'

'Thanks, Da,' said Jack, then he turned and walked out of the room.

CHAPTER TWELVE

Emer felt nervous. She had been waiting for the right moment to approach Miss Clarke, and now the teacher was walking down the street alongside her. It was All Souls' Day, and the pupils of Emer's class were on their way back to the school, having prayed for the dead at a nearby church. The morning was blustery and cold, but Miss Clarke seemed in good spirits, and Emer knew that this was her opportunity.

She took a deep breath, then turned to the teacher. 'I was wondering, Miss …'

'Yes, Emer?'

'I was wondering if you'd like to come to a variety concert next month. I'm playing the piano, and it's to raise money for poor people, coming up to Christmas.'

'That's very commendable. What date is it?'

'December the tenth.'

'That's … that's a Friday, isn't it? Yes, actually, I think I'm free that night,' answered Miss Clarke.

Emer was pleased, but she knew she had to be completely honest. 'There's just one thing, Miss. And if it's a problem, I understand.'

'Now you really have me intrigued – but just a second, Emer,' said the teacher, turning to the line of pupils behind her. 'Careful crossing the road here, girls,' she called, indicating an approaching Guinness dray loaded with wooden barrels and pulled by two huge Clydesdale horses. Miss Clarke supervised the crossing of all the girls, then turned again to Emer as they continued walking towards the school. 'So, what might be a problem?' she asked.

'Well, I hope it won't be,' said Emer, 'but the concert is being run by Conradh na Gaeilge.'

'Why would that be a problem?'

'I thought because you're English, maybe you wouldn't like them being involved.'

Conradh na Gaeilge was an Irish-language organisation that promoted all aspects of Irish culture, but in recent times it had become more openly nationalistic.

'Oh, I think I can risk a concert without turning my back on England's green and pleasant land!' replied Miss Clarke.

'Great,' said Emer.

'Which doesn't mean I'm in sympathy with their politics, not for a moment.'

'OK.'

'But as I've said to you girls in class, it's important we don't all retreat into our own little bubbles.'

'No-one could accuse you of that, Miss.'

'Thank you. But we're all capable of prejudices, Emer. Do you know what the worst thing about prejudice is?'

'What, Miss?'

'The way it hems in our thinking. It's like when someone we're prejudiced against surprises us by doing something good, and instead of being pleased, we're almost annoyed, because now we have to change our view.'

Emer realised that this was true, and it occurred to her that it was conversations like this that made Miss Clarke such an interesting teacher.

'But supposing, Miss, that you're not just prejudiced – but you really disagree with how something is done, or with someone's opinion?'

'Then you pick your battles, Emer. I have to do it all the time.'

'Really?'

'There are so many things wrong in the world. Big things, small things, all sorts of wrongs. You can't fight every battle, so you pick the ones that matter.' Miss Clarke looked at Emer directly. 'It's something you should bear in mind.'

'Do you mean … in school?'

'Everywhere. If you're going to challenge a figure of authority, do it when it really matters, and let other slights go over your head.'

Emer wondered if Miss Clarke was giving her a coded message. 'Do you mean Sister Assumpta?'

'I never mentioned any names!' said Miss Clarke. 'But it's like the Suffragettes, or unions, or any group fighting injustice. You pick the right time to fight your battles. And the right time isn't *every* time.'

Emer was eager to hear more, but before she could ask another question Miss Clarke held up a hand. 'And that's enough of that for now. But thank you for the invitation, Emer. I look forward to your concert.'

Just then they reached the gates of the school, and Emer watched as the teacher shepherded the rest of the girls into the convent.

'That was a great chat you had with Clarkie,' said Joan as Emer entered the schoolyard. 'What was it all about?'

'Good question, Joan,' answered Emer with a wry smile. 'I'm still trying to decide that myself.'

The tall, forbidding walls of Grangegorman Asylum loomed to their right in the heavy November fog as Jack and his mother walked towards Phibsboro. The gas lamps along the street cast small pools of yellow light, and Jack was fascinated by the way the fog made a familiar landscape seem mysterious.

Jack liked Thursday nights when he and Ma walked together to the newsagents in Phibsboro to pay a weekly instalment towards the *Boy's Own* annual that traditionally formed part of his Christmas presents. He enjoyed these companionable strolls with Ma, and she always bought him a toffee bar in the newsagents as part of their routine.

They walked on through the swirling fog, with vehicles and other pedestrians materialising and then disappearing, and Jack let his mind drift. It was three weeks now since the fight with Phelim O'Connell, and there had been surprisingly little fallout at school in its aftermath. Brother McGill had accepted Da's assurance that Jack would be punished and hadn't pushed matters any further. Most of the boys in the class felt that Jack had won fair and square, and Gerry Quinn had overheard friends of Phelim's saying that he was embarrassed by his parents' intervention, even though the split lip had genuinely prevented him from playing football for the school. At any rate Phelim had made no further reference to it, and Jack had been happy for them to keep their distance from each other and just get on with things.

Thinking of Gerry Quinn, Jack looked at Ma now, unsure how to phrase what he had in mind. They were approaching the junction with Cabra Road, and the huge Gothic spire of St Peter's Church towered above them, its upper section disappearing into the fog. Jack waited until they were safely across the road, having deftly avoided a coalman's cart that suddenly came clattering out of the gloom, before turning to his mother.

'I was just thinking, Ma,' he said.

'Yes?' she answered encouragingly.

'You remember Gerry Quinn, the boy from my class that we gave the clothes to?'

Ma nodded. 'Poor mite, living with a drunk of an uncle.'

'He has it tough, all right. And he just told me he's giving up school next year.'

'Really?'

'He'll be thirteen in February, so once he finishes primary school, his uncle will take him out and make him work.'

'God love him.'

'Yeah. So I was thinking. Could we maybe put something aside each week at the newsagents for Gerry too? I'd give some of my pocket money towards it.'

'What had you got in mind?'

'Maybe the *Chums* annual? Or *The Wonder Book of Railways*? He's a bit proud, so normally he mightn't want to take anything. But if we said it was a farewell present because he's leaving school, he'd probably take it then.'

Ma stopped walking and looked at Jack.

'What?'

Ma reached out and touched his cheek. 'You're a good lad, Jack. Da and me, we must have done something right!'

'Does that mean we can do it?'

'With the girls working as well as your da, we're more comfortable than we've ever been. So it's only right we share our good fortune.'

'Thanks, Ma, that's great.'

'Poor lad,' said Ma as they continued on their way. 'His only hope was an education. He'll never get a decent job now.'

'It's really unfair,' said Jack. 'He started off poor, he's still poor and he'll always be poor.'

'That's the way of the world, Jack.'

'But it shouldn't be. Maybe Mr Davey isn't so wrong after all, Ma. Maybe we do need a bit of a revolution.'

Ma stopped suddenly. She looked Jack directly in the eye,

her cheeks rosy and her face animated against the backdrop of white fog.

'No, Jack, don't make that mistake. Violence won't help the Gerry Quinns of this world. When I was your age, there was a secret society in Dublin called The Invincibles. Have you heard of them?'

'Yes, they … they killed people in the Phoenix Park.'

'They murdered the Chief Secretary and Under Secretary for Ireland in broad daylight. The two most senior British officials in Ireland, stabbed to death in view of the Viceregal Lodge. The Invincibles claimed they were Irish nationalists, but all their violence achieved was to kill two innocent men and get themselves hanged. To say nothing of putting Home Rule back by about thirty years. Don't listen to Mr Davey, or Emer, or anyone who tells you that violence is the answer. All right?'

'Yes, Ma.'

'We have to have law and order. And even though voting to change things is slow, it's the only way people like Gerry might get their chance one day. Do you understand?'

It wasn't often that Ma spoke as forcefully as this, but Jack found it all the more convincing now that she had.

'Yes, Ma,' he said. 'I understand.'

'Good boy,' she answered, then her tone changed and she winked at him. 'Right, let's go pay our instalments – for two annuals!'

'Two annuals it is!' replied Jack, then they headed off again through the foggy city streets.

'Ladies and gentlemen, I have a question for you all,' said Ben, pretending to be a master of ceremonies.

They were on the upper deck of a tram taking them home from swimming training, and everyone was in good spirits. The teams for the gala had been announced, and Emer had made the first team, as she had hoped. She was almost as pleased for Jack, though, who had achieved his goal of gaining one of the places on the last boys' team.

Emer turned smilingly to Ben. 'So, what's the question?'

'The question is: what's the jelly-looking stuff between sharks' teeth called?'

'I hope this isn't disgusting,' said Gladys.

'Relax, will you?' said Ben to his sister.

'OK,' said Jack, 'what *is* the jelly-looking stuff between sharks' teeth?'

'Slow swimmers!'

Everybody laughed, although Gladys nevertheless reprimanded her brother. 'It is still kind of disgusting, Ben. Where did you hear it?'

'In the baths tonight. I heard the captain telling one of the coaches during training.'

'Talking about the captain,' said Joan, 'did you ever notice his knees? They're really bockety-looking!'

Joan, Ben and Gladys started what Emer thought was a pretty silly discussion about the captain's knees. After a moment she turned to Jack, with whom she was sharing the seat. 'Congratulations again on making the team.'

'Thanks.'

'You've come a long way from not wanting to put your face in the water!'

'I suppose I have. All thanks to you.'

'I just pointed you in the right direction. You got on the team yourself.'

'Well, either way, thanks, Emer.'

'You're grand. Though now you mention it, maybe you could do me a favour.'

'What is it?'

'It's really funny when you do your version of "When Father Papered the Parlour". Would you sing it at a fundraising concert I'm playing in next month?'

Jack hesitated, and Emer pressed on. 'Say you will, Jack. We need more performers.'

'And what are you fundraising for?'

'To help poor people coming up to Christmas. It's being organised by Conradh na Gaeilge – but don't worry, there won't be any politics. It's just a charity concert.'

'Well … OK, then.'

'You're a star!'

'I'll still have to ask at home,' said Jack. 'But seeing as it's for charity, I'd say it'll be all right.'

'Great.'

'I'll need to practise, though, to sing in public.'

'Me too. I'm doing a Chopin nocturne.'

'Right.'

'So we'll both practise our pieces, and we'll both practise our swimming. And then we'll win the gala and dazzle them at the concert! How does that sound?'

'Sounds good.'

'Right so, that's that,' said Emer, then she sat back contentedly as the tram rattled along the tracks and carried them through the night.

CHAPTER THIRTEEN

Jack bit his tongue, trying not to let his impatience show. His sister Mary usually meant well, but she could be annoyingly bossy, and Jack felt that he didn't need his sixteen-year-old sister to act as a babysitter.

His other sisters were out, and his parents had gone to town to visit a music hall. Jack had been working away at his fretwork in the warmth of the kitchen, building a wooden replica of Dublin's Custom House. Now, though, Mary was acting like a know-all and pointing at his handiwork.

'You need to sand that down a bit more, Jack. Then it will take the paint better.'

'Really?'

'Yeah. And you should wedge the base to make it more stable.'

'When did you become a carpenter?' asked Jack.

'Don't be smart, I'm just trying to help. And I'm not a carpenter, but I've learnt lots of mechanical stuff in the factory.'

'You might know about making shells, but–'

'Not just shells,' interjected Mary. 'I've learnt loads of things. They claimed that women couldn't run factories, but they were wrong. It said in the paper last week that since the men went off to war and women replaced them, production has more than doubled.'

Jack had actually heard this, so he couldn't argue back.

'The powers-that-be got that dead wrong,' said Mary. 'Lots of other stuff too.'

'Like what?'

'Well … like this plan for conscription. The government says married men won't be conscripted into the army until young, unmarried men have been called up first.'

'Well, does that not kind of make sense?' asked Jack. 'I mean, married men have families.'

'Just because you're lucky enough to meet someone, get married and have a family – why should you have preference in not getting called up? That's not right.'

'I, eh … I hadn't thought of it like that,' said Jack. 'But at least they're not bringing in conscription in Ireland.'

'Not so far,' corrected Mary.

'Yeah,' conceded Jack. Although there was huge opposition to the idea of conscription in Ireland, the government in Westminster needed troops to replace the catastrophic losses. It had long been a worry for Jack that despite his job as a policeman, Da might get called up.

Before they could take the conversation further, Jack heard the front door opening, then Ma and Da came down the hall and entered the kitchen.

They were in great form after their night out, and everyone exchanged greetings as Jack's parents took off their overcoats and warmed themselves at the range. Da enthused about some of the music hall acts they had seen, and Jack felt that this was a good cue.

'Talking about music halls, Da,' he said, 'is it OK if I appear in a variety concert?'

'Doing what?'

'Singing "When Father Papered the Parlour".'

'Are you going professional?' said Ma playfully.

'No, it's just a fundraising concert to help poor people coming up to Christmas.'

'Very good,' said Da. 'And who asked you?'

'Emer. She's playing the piano in it. It's being run by Conradh na Gaeilge, but there's no politics – it's just for charity.'

'I see,' said Da.

'It's on December the tenth. Will you and Ma come?'

Da shook his head. 'I'm afraid not, Jack. I'd like to help a charity, and I know you say it's not political. But Conradh na Gaeilge has become more political lately, and I've a new Inspector who's really strict. So I can't be seen to support something like this.'

Jack was surprised at his father's response. His disappointment must have shown, because Da reached out and squeezed his arm sympathetically.

'I know at times it's hard being a policeman's son, Jack. And I know you're going to be disappointed, but I'm sorry, you can't be involved with this either.'

'Ah, Da.'

'Emer is a nice girl, and the Daveys are lovely people. But Mr

Davey is an officer in the Volunteers. If trouble comes – and it may well – I can't have anyone in the force pointing a finger and saying our family is involved with rebels.'

Jack was taken aback. 'So are you saying … Are you saying I can't be friends with Emer?'

'No, of course not,' said Da. 'You can still be pals, you can go to their house, you can be friendly with Mr and Mrs Davey. But anything to do with the Volunteers or Conradh na Gaeilge – that's not on.'

Jack was bitterly disappointed, and he looked appealingly to his mother.

'I'm sorry, Jack,' she said, 'but Da's right. The DMP is our livelihood, and it can't be put at risk. You'll have to talk to Emer and tell her you're pulling out of this concert.'

'Sorry, son,' said Da, 'but that's the way it is. All right?'

Jack felt like crying, but he kept his tears at bay, nodded agreement to his father, then turned away and wordlessly began work again on his model of the Custom House.

Emer released some of her frustration as she booted the wayward football back to where the local boys were playing further up the street. Earlier the boys and girls had had a game of rounders together, and now Ben and Jack were playing in an impromptu soccer match, while Emer and Gladys made their way down

Ellesmere Avenue towards the Phoenix Park.

Joan was visiting her aunt, but Emer and Gladys had decided to go to hear a brass band play in the park. It was a mild Sunday afternoon in late November, and the city was bathed in a golden glow of hazy sunshine, but Emer's mood was at odds with the mellow atmosphere. 'Sometimes Mam makes me want to scream,' she said.

'Yeah?' answered Gladys.

'I mean, she didn't even bat an eyelid. She just said, "Oh, you'll have to skip this swimming gala, it clashes with dancing in the *céilí mór.*"'

'I thought you liked Irish dancing.'

'It's good fun, but I'm never going to win any medals for it. I could win something at the gala, though. And I've been training hard. It's really annoying.'

Gladys nodded sympathetically. 'It's a pity. But you do a lot of stuff, Emer. Now and then things are going to clash.'

'Sometimes I wish I was like you and Ben.'

'How do you mean?'

'Not an only child.'

Gladys looked surprised. 'Really?'

'Mam and Dad follow everything I do. Irish classes, dancing, piano, swimming, elocution – they follow my every move!'

'You're not the only one, Emer.'

'I am the only one! All the rest of you have brothers or sisters.'

'I mean you're not the only one whose parents interfere. Sure mine are the same. And look at Jack. He has four sisters, and his mam and dad still check up on him – like the way they stopped him singing in the concert.'

'That was really stupid. We live in Ireland, but they're terrified of doing anything that shows them as Irish!'

'So it's not just your parents, Emer.'

'No. But mine are the opposite. Everything Irish comes first.'

'Right.'

'Don't get me wrong,' said Emer. 'I'm still for independence and the Volunteers and all. I just think everything else shouldn't have to be dropped.'

'Could you not persuade them? You're usually pretty good at arguing.'

They turned onto the North Circular Road, which was busy with cars, horses and carriages as Dubliners made for the oasis of the Phoenix Park.

'I tried,' Emer answered, 'but they really want me to do the céilí, so it would have been a major battle.'

'You're usually not afraid of that.'

'I know. But Miss Clarke in school said something that made me think.'

'What?' asked Gladys.

'She told me you have to pick your battles. That you can't win every fight, so you pick the ones that matter.'

'And this one doesn't?'

'I'd really like to do the gala, but I think there'll be bigger battles ahead.'

'Do you mean … with the Volunteers and the government and all?'

Emer nodded. 'They don't want me involved, but I need to be part of it. There has to be something I can do.' She saw that her friend looked worried, so she smiled. 'Don't worry, Gladys. It's not going to happen today or tomorrow.'

'But if it does happen?'

'I have to be in it.'

'Right.'

'Meanwhile, though, let's forget about all this trouble. Let's get ice creams at the park gates and listen to the band, OK?'

'OK,' said Gladys.

'Good,' said Emer, then she smiled again at her friend and strolled on in the winter sunshine.

CHAPTER FOURTEEN

Jack loved the contrasts of December; the freezing schoolyard glistened with frost, while the classroom felt cosy, with a roaring turf fire going in the grate. Brother McGill was in a relaxed mood today. Their religious instruction class had consisted of an advent talk, in which he had encouraged his pupils to get into the right frame of mind for Christmas. Earlier he had allowed Jack to share a large box of sweets amongst his classmates, a move that had boosted Jack's popularity.

The sweets had been donated by the captain of Jack's swimming club to celebrate their victory in the gala the previous Friday night. Being on the winning team had delighted Jack, and now, as he sucked the last sweet sliver of one of the toffees, he marvelled at how unpredictable life could be.

Less than five months ago he had nearly drowned because he wasn't a strong swimmer, yet since then he had improved so much that he had won a place on a swimming team. On the negative side, however, his parents had unexpectedly stopped him from performing in Emer's charity concert, and Emer's parents had stopped her from taking part in the gala. Then there had been another positive, when the gala outcome had been balanced on a knife-edge and they had won in the final race.

'All right, lunch break,' said Brother McGill now as the bell sounded in the schoolyard outside their window. The teacher quickly gathered his papers into his leather satchel. 'Right, lads, see you all at two o'clock sharp!' he said and exited the class-room.

The class immediately began to break up, and Gerry Quinn turned to Jack and indicated the departing teacher. 'Did you hear what Giller keeps in that satchel?' he asked.

'No, what?'

'Whacker Moran in 6B peeked into it when Giller was called out of the classroom last Friday.'

'What was in it?' asked Jack, his curiosity aroused.

'A cowboys and Indians book. *Massacre at Fort Apache*. Imagine Giller reading something like that!'

Jack smiled. Even though it seemed at odds with the teacher's enthusiasm for all things Irish, somehow he *could* imagine him reading an adventure about cowboys and Indians. 'He probably pictures himself leading the US cavalry,' said Jack.

'Yeah,' agreed Gerry, 'laying into the Apaches with *Seán Dubh*!'

Jack laughed, then his smile faded as Phelim O'Connell approached them.

'Wanted a word, Madigan,' he said. 'On your own.'

'Don't start anything,' Gerry warned the other boy.

'It's OK, Gerry,' said Jack quietly. 'I can handle it.'

'Fine,' said Gerry, moving off and leaving Jack alone with Phelim.

Jack wondered what Phelim was planning, and he tensed himself, ready for action if need be. In the weeks since their fight they had stayed out of each other's way – if anything, Jack felt that maybe Phelim respected him for standing up for himself. Then again, maybe the bigger boy wanted revenge for his split lip and had been biding his time to lull Jack into a false sense of security.

After Da being so understanding about the fight, Jack really wanted to avoid another incident, and so he kept his tone neutral when he spoke. 'So, what is it you wanted?'

Phelim said nothing for the moment, and Jack realised that he was waiting for the boys nearby to leave. Phelim stared hard at a couple of them, and they quickly got the message.

Jack balanced himself on the balls of his feet, hoping to avoid trouble but ready in case Phelim tried to catch him unawares with a blow.

'I've been thinking,' said Phelim.

'Yeah?' answered Jack. The other boy's tone wasn't aggressive, but Jack stayed on guard, wary in case Phelim tried to trick him. He could see a tiny mark where Phelim's lip had been split, but he shifted his gaze to his eyes, ready for any hint of an attack.

'I've been thinking,' repeated Phelim, 'about what Giller said.'

'Giller said a lot of things.'

'About Christmas. And the season of goodwill. And I thought … maybe we should bury the hatchet.'

Jack was dumbfounded. *Could this be some kind of ruse?* He stayed on the balls of his feet, still ready to react. But Phelim seemed to be speaking sincerely.

'I'm still against the British Army and the DMP and all that, but ... well, I shouldn't have said what I did about your cousin.'

Jack stared at him, amazed and not knowing what to say.

'So when Giller said Christmas is a time to right wrongs, I thought ... maybe we should just accept we're on different sides and leave it at that. OK?'

Jack was still wary, but he nodded. 'OK.'

'We don't have to pretend to be pals. But ... well, we could try to get along.' Phelim tentatively reached out and offered a hand-shake. 'What do you say?'

Jack hesitated for a moment, then remembering what had been said about goodwill and peace on earth, he held out his own hand and shook Phelim's. The bigger boy held his handshake for a moment, then nodded in farewell and walked out of the classroom.

Jack stood unmoving. Earlier he had marvelled at life's unpredictability, but this was the most surprising thing of all. He smiled to himself, wondered what other surprises lay in store, then gathered his schoolbag and left the room with a spring in his step.

'It's simply appalling, girls,' said Miss Clarke, 'that the Ku Klux Klan has been revived in Georgia.'

It was coming to the end of the history lesson, Emer's final class of the day, but as usual the teacher had made the subject so interesting that Emer wanted the class to go on.

'The Ku Klux Klan is violently opposed to black people, Catholics, Jews and immigrants,' said Miss Clarke. 'So what does history teach us about dealing with such a threat?'

Joan raised her hand.

'Yes, Joan?'

'That we try to see their viewpoint, Miss?'

'Normally that would be the case. As, for example, when I went to Emer's concert that was run by Conradh na Gaeilge. If you don't mind me using that as an example, Emer?'

'No, Miss,' said Emer.

'As an Englishwoman, I don't necessarily agree with the stance taken recently by Conradh na Gaeilge,' continued the teacher. 'But I went to Emer's concert – at which, may I say, Emer, you played very well.'

'Thanks, Miss,' answered Emer, surprised but pleased that her piano playing had found its way into a history lesson.

'As I say, I went to Emer's concert and exchanged views with many people afterwards – some of them moderate Irish nationalists, some of them fervent nationalists. That, girls, is a healthy thing, where people of differing opinions exchange views and try to see each other's standpoints.'

'So why can't we do that with the Ku Klux Klan, Miss?' asked Joan.

'Because some things are just so wrong they mustn't be indulged. You can't have a reasoned argument with somebody who would lynch a black man – brutally hang him from a tree – simply because of the colour of his skin. Some wrongs are so blatant they must be firmly rejected.'

Just then the bell rang to mark the end of the school day, and Miss Clarke closed her folder. 'To be continued, girls,' she said. 'Class dismissed.'

There was a flurry of activity. Emer and Joan packed their schoolbags, then left the classroom together and sauntered down the corridor.

'So what was Clarkie really like at the concert?' asked Joan. 'Did your mam and dad think she was mad?'

'No, actually, they thought she was great.'

'Really? Even though she's English?'

'They're not against ordinary English people, Joan. Just the ones who rule us.'

'Right.'

'It was all very polite, and herself and Dad agreed to disagree about the Volunteers. But she was all in favour of Conradh na Gaeilge promoting the Irish language, so that went down well.'

'Adults are weird!' said Joan. 'You can never tell what they'll do. Oops, Creeper alert!'

Emer looked up to see Sister Assumpta approaching down the corridor. The two girls courteously greeted the nun, who nodded in acknowledgement as she passed.

'Look at the face on her,' whispered Joan. 'It would stop a clock!'

'Yeah. Not exactly in the Christmas spirit, is she?'

'Well, that's the thing,' answered Joan. 'Maybe she *is*, in her own way.'

Emer looked at her friend curiously. 'How do you mean?'

'Marie Gogan saw her giving half a crown to a beggar in town.'

'Really? Half a crown?'

'Yeah. Marie was shopping with her mother, but Creeper didn't see her. And there was this old man begging, and he had only one leg. And Creeper stopped and gave him half a crown. So maybe she's not all bad.'

'No,' said Emer thoughtfully. 'So she makes our lives a misery in here, and she's dead generous outside. You're right – adults *are* weird!'

Jack watched carefully as Da filled his pipe with tobacco. He wanted to make his move while Da was relaxed, and he was always at his most approachable when sitting in the armchair by the fire with a good pipe going. Ma and Sheila were at the living-room table, putting the finishing touches to an elaborate hat they were making. Maureen and Mary were out, Una was reading the newspaper, and Jack was carefully painting the railings of his fretwork model of the Custom House.

'A new cinema has opened on Sackville Street,' said Una, reading excitedly from the paper. 'It's called the Carlton, and it will hold six hundred people.'

'You're a divil for the cinema,' said Da as he struck a match, then he puffed away to get his pipe going.

'Why not?' said Una. 'Myself and Mary work hard. After a week making shells, we're entitled to some entertainment.'

'God forbid that you wouldn't be entertained!' said Ma, looking up from her hat-making with a grin. 'I don't know what I did for entertainment at your age when there were no cinemas.'

'Times change, Ma,' answered Una.

'They do,' said Da, 'and not always for the better.'

'Ah, Da, that sounds like a real old man's thing to say!' said Sheila with a laugh.

As the eldest and most sensible of Jack's sisters, Sheila could get away with saying things that the rest of them couldn't, and Jack watched now as Da smiled benignly.

'Sure, I *am* an old man,' he said. 'Well – almost!'

The pipe smoke had a sweet, comforting smell, and Jack sensed that now was the moment to make his request. 'I was wondering, Da,' he said, putting down his paint brush.

'Were you now? And what were you wondering?'

'Ben and Gladys and Joan and Emer are all going down to Monasterevin to a Christmas fair. Emer's uncle lives there, and they're going down on the train, staying overnight with the uncle and coming back the next day. Can I go too, please?'

His father took the pipe from his mouth. 'I don't know about that, Jack.'

'Please, Da. This time it's nothing to do with Conradh na Gaeilge or the Volunteers, it's just a Christmas outing.' Jack suspected that his parents felt bad about refusing him permission to sing in Emer's concert, and he hoped now that they might balance things out by letting him go.

'Why would you want to go to Monasterevin?' asked Una.

'Because my friends are all going, and it would be great fun.'

'And what adult is in charge?' asked Ma.

Jack thought it was encouraging that Ma wasn't rejecting the proposal out of hand. 'Mrs Davey will bring everyone to the station,' he said. 'We'd travel down on the train, and Emer's uncle would collect everyone at the station in Monasterevin.'

'Right.'

'I'd love to go, Ma. Please, can I?'

His mother looked across to where Da sat at the fireplace and raised an eyebrow in enquiry. Jack held his breath as his father put down his pipe.

'I don't want to be a killjoy, Jack,' he said. 'But like I told you, our new Inspector is very strict. "Fraternising with undesirables", he calls it.'

'In fairness, Da,' said Una, 'you could hardly call the Daveys undesirables!'

'Not as neighbours, no, of course not. But politically …'

'But politics hardly comes into it, Da,' said Sheila. 'It's just a group of kids going to a Christmas fair.'

Jack had been just about to make the same argument. But Da respected Sheila's responsible approach to life, so Jack decided it would be better to say nothing and let his sister make the argument for him.

'And besides,' continued Sheila. 'The Inspector will never know. Like Jack said, it's nothing to do with the Volunteers. It's just a group of friends going down the country for one night.'

Jack felt a surge of affection for his big sister. He turned to look at his father.

For a moment Da said nothing, then he breathed out resignedly and nodded. 'All right then. But keep it to yourself, Jack. Don't broadcast to all and sundry that you're a guest of the Daveys, all right?'

'I'm sworn to silence, Da! Wild horses wouldn't get it out of me!'

The others laughed, then Jack thanked his parents, gave Sheila a grateful nod and went contentedly back to painting his model.

CHAPTER FIFTEEN

Emer thought Monasterevin was wonderful. It had a fascinating network of waterways and bridges, with the River Barrow, the Grand Canal, the Great Southern Railway and the Portarlington branch of the canal all coming together in this small County Kildare town.

Emer's uncle Peadar and his wife, Gertie, had no children of their own, but they made Emer and her pals feel really welcome. They lived in an old house close to the lock-keeper's cottage on the canal. Emer had enjoyed her friends' excitement earlier in the day when the nearby lifting bridge had allowed a barge to cross the Barrow, the boat suspended high above the river on a narrow stone aqueduct.

As part of the Christmas fair, coloured lights had been installed along Monasterevin's streets, attached to the walls of the tall canal warehouses. Now as Emer looked out the window of her uncle's cosy kitchen at the night sky, a swirl of snowflakes was falling, giving the streets a fairy-tale quality.

Emer cradled a mug of homemade broth in her hands as she turned back to her friends, who were all seated at the kitchen table. Uncle Peadar and Aunt Gertie had retreated to the parlour with Mr Cronin, a local bargeman and a friend of her uncle's, leaving the five friends to sing songs and tell ghost stories around a crackling log fire. Even the novelty of drinking soup from tin mugs instead of the more usual soup bowls made the night seem special. Emer had suggested to Jack that they might extend their circle and ask Gerry to join them for this trip, but the other boy was working flat out selling Christmas trees door-to-door with his uncle.

'Wouldn't it be brilliant if the snow got heavy and we had it for Christmas?' asked Gladys as the falling snowflakes lightly dusted the gaunt branches of the trees outside the kitchen window.

Jack nodded in agreement. 'Yeah, like you see in the Christmas cards.'

'I'd rather if it snowed in January, when we're back at school,' said Joan.

Ben looked at her in surprise. 'Why?'

'Because the pipes might freeze, and we'd get off school! It's no good if they freeze when we're on holidays.'

'So that's your Christmas wish – that the pipes freeze?' asked Ben.

Joan laughed. 'No, that's my January wish!'

'We should all pick what we'd like if there was no limit and we could each have one wish come true,' suggested Emer.

'Has it to be something that could really happen, though?' asked Gladys.

Ben looked at his sister. 'She just said there's no limit.'

'I know, but I'm just asking … Is it dream stuff, like being a queen, or is it a wish for something real?'

'It can be anything you like, Gladys,' answered Emer. 'So who wants to go first?'

'Why don't you go,' suggested Jack, 'seeing as it's your idea?'

Emer considered it for a moment. 'I think I'd like to live in a castle on the Rhine for a year. And then come back to find Ireland was an independent republic!'

'Come on, that's two wishes, Emer!' said Ben.

'OK, well you can limit yourself to one!'

Ben looked thoughtful. 'Eh … my wish would be to be a professional cricket player.'

'Good choice, Ben,' said Jack.

'And what about you, Jack?' asked Emer.

'I'd be given a private tour by the Commissioner behind the scenes in Scotland Yard.'

'Brilliant. And Gladys?'

'I'm not certain. But I think I'd like to visit my pen friend in Wales.'

'That's a really boring wish!' said Ben.

'No more boring than you and your aul' cricket!' answered his sister.

'And what about you, Joan?' asked Emer.

'I'd like to inherit a chocolate factory!'

The others laughed, then Emer looked up as her Aunt Gertie came into the room.

'OK, it's getting late. Time for bed,' said Gertie.

'Ten more minutes?' asked Emer. 'Please?'

Aunt Gertie laughed. 'All right, miss! Ten more minutes, then bed for everyone.'

'Thanks,' said Emer. She looked back at her friends and winked, happy to savour every last minute of this magical winter's night.

Jack sat up in bed, trying not to make a sound. He was sharing a bedroom with Ben, and they were directly above the parlour. The old wooden boards of the bedroom floor had some gaps, and Jack could see shafts of light from the room below. More importantly, he could hear Emer's uncle Peadar and his friend Mr Cronin through the floor, and their conversation had made him sit up attentively.

Ben had drifted off to sleep within minutes of their candle being extinguished. Normally Jack had no trouble sleeping either, but the combination of a strange room and an action-packed day was keeping his mind active. The train journey to Monasterevin had been great fun, and Jack had thoroughly enjoyed the Christmas fair, which featured carol-singing and food and drink stalls with free samples. Rather than being sleepy after a busy day, however, he had tossed and turned for a long time. But now he was wide awake.

It hadn't come as a surprise that Emer's uncle Peadar was a nationalist – after all, he was the brother of Mr Davey, who was a captain in the Volunteers – but Jack had still been fascinated when he first heard Uncle Peadar and Mr Cronin discussing the delivery of a secret consignment of 'supplies'. It was clear that the two men thought they weren't being overheard, and it sounded increasingly to Jack as though the supplies were for the Volunteers.

He remained stock still in his bed now, afraid that any movement might alert the men in the room below. In truth they were probably too caught up in what they were doing to be listening out for sounds from the bedroom, but Jack didn't want to take any chances.

Just then there was a tapping on the window of the parlour below, and Jack heard Peadar saying, 'That'll be him'. This was followed by the sound of a chair being pulled back as Emer's uncle rose from his seat and made for the hall. Jack heard the front door creaking open and being gently shut, and then Mr Cronin greeted the newcomer as he came into the parlour.

'Good man, Dinny,' he said. 'Everything go well?'

'No hitches,' answered the man called Dinny.

'Where are you moored?' asked Peadar.

Jack suspected that Dinny must have transported the secret consignment to Monasterevin by barge, and he listened carefully for the answer.

'In the shadows at the far warehouse.'

'Right, let's get it safely stowed away,' said Peadar.

The men started for the hall again. Jack remained unmoving, but his mind was racing. What was the right thing to do? The easy solution would be to say nothing and try to go back to sleep. But that would be a coward's way out. Should he try to alert the local police? But that would feel like a betrayal, especially after having eavesdropped in a house in which he was a guest. And besides, he couldn't say for certain that the supplies were weapons or ammunition. *Unless I check it out.*

Jack bit his lip, unsure what to do. Then he followed his instincts, slipped back the blankets and swung his feet out onto the floor. He would need to be fast to keep the men in sight, but he couldn't risk waking Ben. Moving quietly but swiftly, he pulled his trousers and sweater on over his pyjamas, slipped his feet into his shoes and quickly tied the laces.

He tiptoed to the bedroom door and crept down the stairs. Reaching the front door, he opened it carefully to minimise its creaky sound, then stepped out into the winter night and closed the door gently behind him. The snowfall had stopped, but a light dusting of powdery snow lay on the ground and reflected the soft-coloured light from the lanterns attached to the nearby warehouse walls. In the faint glow Jack could make out Peadar leading Dinny and Cronin down the street.

Jack shivered in the sudden cold, then followed them, figuring that later on he could get back into the house through the back door, which the men had left unlocked. They were on the edge of town here, and Jack encountered nobody on the street at this time of night. Striding quietly, he narrowed the gap between himself and the men, then came to a sudden halt when he saw that they had stopped at one of the furthest warehouses. They were past the last of the coloured lanterns, but Jack could still make out the figure of Peadar opening the warehouse door. Simultaneously Dinny moved to the deck of a long boat that was barely visible, moored as it was in the shadows opposite the warehouse.

Jack flattened himself against a wall and watched a faint glow from inside the warehouse. He realised that Emer's uncle must have lit a small candle, then he saw Dinny and Cronin carrying a wooden box each and making for the warehouse.

Still keeping to the wall, Jack drew nearer. He was getting his night vision now, and he could make out shapes on the deck of the barge that he suspected to be the rest of the supplies that the men planned to unload. The boxes were clearly heavy, so it would take a while to move them all. If he timed it right, he might be able to board the boat and check the boxes while the men were inside. *If I time it right*. But what if he got it wrong and they caught him? The Volunteers regarded themselves as an army – and Jack was well aware of what armies did to spies. He shivered, and he knew it wasn't just from the cold. But he had come this far, and he couldn't just walk away.

Just then the three men emerged from the warehouse, and each of them took another box from the deck of the barge. Jack waited until they crossed back to the warehouse entrance, then he sprinted towards the vessel. He assumed that they were storing the goods somewhere inside the building, but he didn't know how long he would have before they came out for the next load. He lightly jumped up on the deck of the barge, then bent down to try to read the lettering that was on the outside of the boxes. With the door of the warehouse closed over, there was hardly any light spill, and Jack couldn't read the wording. He decided to lift one of the lids. If he opened a box and found bullets or sticks of dynamite, he would have his proof. *And then what will I do?* He didn't know, but until he was sure of the boxes' contents, nothing could be decided.

The lid of the box was firmly closed, and before Jack could find a way to open it, the door of the warehouse swung ajar. Jack immediately dropped behind the stack of wooden boxes and froze. He heard the men approaching – sooner than he had expected – and he felt his heart pounding in his chest.

It occurred to him that he had wiped snow off the top of the box while trying to open the lid, and he cursed himself. *What was I thinking?!* If the men were alert, they might notice that someone had been at one of the boxes. And any kind of a search would reveal his hiding place, mere yards from where the men were now.

Jack stayed totally still and held his breath. If the worst came to the worst and his hiding place was discovered, he would dive into the canal and swim for the far bank. The water would be freezing, but if he escaped into the darkness on the far side, he might be able to get back to the house and jump into bed without his face being seen. It was a desperate plan, and it would backfire completely if they saw his face. *Or if they shot me in the back while I swam across the canal.* There was every reason to suspect that men moving an important secret consignment would be armed. Before he could worry about it any more, the men reached the barge.

'Damn it, lads,' whispered Dinny. 'Look.'

Jack prayed that he wasn't referring to the box with the snow removed. He pressed his knees together to stop them from shaking.

'What is it?' asked Peadar.

Jack felt like his chest would explode from the tension as he waited for Dinny to answer.

'The moon,' whispered the bargeman. 'It's going to come out from behind the clouds.'

Jack felt a surge of relief, then realised he wasn't out of trouble yet. Just as Dinny had predicted, the moon suddenly came out from behind the clouds, brightening the scene. Jack wondered if any part of his body would be visible now. But even if it was, he couldn't risk moving, with the men only a few feet away.

'Right, let's speed this up!' said Peadar.

Jack heard a grunt as Emer's uncle lifted one of the heavy boxes, then Dinny followed suit. There was a short pause, and Jack's mind started racing. Had Cronin spotted the snow-cleared box? Or Jack's footprints on the snow-dusted deck, visible now in the moonlight? It was as though time stood still, and the couple of seconds before Cronin went into action seemed like an eternity to Jack. Then the man breathed out heavily as he hoisted a box and hurried after his companions.

Jack let his breath out slowly before rising into a crouch. He needed to get off the barge quickly, especially now that the men were moving at a faster pace because of the brighter conditions. He also realised that this was his chance to read the writing on the boxes. He moved swiftly back to the front of the barge, and there, in the moonlight, he read the lettering on the top box: 'Dynamite – handle with extreme care!'

Well that answers my question and no mistake, he thought, then he jumped down from the boat onto the bank. He knew that the men could return from the warehouse any second, and so he sprinted away, keeping to the shadows and not stopping till he turned around a corner out of sight. This street too was brightened by moonlight, but Jack retreated further into the shadows and tried to gather his wits. His heart was still racing from his near-discovery, and he breathed deeply, trying to think clearly.

The law-abiding thing to do would be to report all of this to the police. But that would result in Emer's uncle being arrested and would feel like a betrayal of Emer – while he was a guest of her family. Yet if he did nothing, the Volunteers would have dynamite, and that could mean people getting killed.

He knew that Emer would argue that countless thousands of people were already being killed on the Western Front and in the Dardanelles, and that the authorities didn't seem too concerned about that. And there was also her argument – which Jack found hard to dispute – that the British Government had allowed the Ulster Volunteer Force to arm themselves to the teeth, and that the Irish Volunteers had to have weapons to defend themselves in the event of a civil war.

He didn't know how long he had been standing there on the street, conflicting thoughts going around in his mind, but suddenly he realised that he was shivering badly. The realisation brought him to his senses – he had to get back to the bedroom. And not just before he caught a chill, but also before Peadar and Cronin returned. He still didn't know whether or not to report what he had seen, but either way he couldn't stay here. He turned on his heel, stepped out of the shadows and started briskly back.

CHAPTER SIXTEEN

Emer applauded vigorously as the curtain came down on the brightly lit stage for the intermission of the Christmas pantomime. She was in the Dress Circle of Dublin's Gaiety Theatre with her parents, and she was wearing the new blue dress that Mam had bought as her Christmas outfit. Emer loved the dress, and her parents were also smartly turned out, in keeping with the glamour of the occasion. Emer loved all the traditions of Christmas but particularly the family's annual visit to the pantomime the day after St Stephen's Day. This year the Gaiety's production of *Dick Whittington* featured the Marigny troupe of Lady Dancers as well as a band, chorus and ballet, and Emer had thoroughly enjoyed it.

On Christmas Eve they had travelled by train to stay for two days with Dad's family in County Kildare. Emer liked seeing her cousins and aunts and uncles, but she missed her friends. Before setting off for the station she had swapped presents with Gladys, Ben, Jack and Joan. Gladys had given her a lovely pair of kid gloves, Ben had surprised her with a chemistry set – a strange choice, but one about which she politely enthused – Jack had given her the *Girl's Own* annual, and Joan's gift was a large box of fancy toffees.

Having her friends to stay overnight in Aunt Gertie and Uncle

Peadar's the previous week had been great fun, and a snowy Monasterevin had looked magical the next morning. All in all, Emer reckoned that this was turning out to be one of the best Christmases ever.

'Think you could force yourself to have a glass of lemonade?' her father asked playfully as they rose from their seats and headed out of the Dress Circle.

'I'll do my very best, Dad,' answered Emer with mock seriousness.

'Brave girl!' said Mam with a laugh, and they made their way along the carpeted corridor to the bar. All the patrons around them were dressed in their finery, and it struck Emer that Mam and Dad were actually a handsome couple.

Her father intercepted one of the barmen who was crossing the room with a tray of drinks and placed their order. Emer stood with her parents just inside the door of the bar, since all of the tables were occupied. She consulted her programme, eagerly scanning the list of performers. 'Would you say there'll be an escape artist in Act Two, Mam?' she asked. 'Or maybe a juggler?'

'Have to wait and see, love.'

'There was an escape artist in Act One,' said Dad.

Emer looked at her father disbelievingly. 'No, there wasn't.'

'That fella who sang "Mother Machree" was an escape artist. The way he butchered the song, he was lucky to escape with his life!'

'Eamon,' said Mam reproachfully, but she was laughing as she said it.

Emer loved when Dad was in good humour like this. Between running two grocery shops and being in the Volunteers, he was kept very busy, but when he relaxed he was good company. Emer always thought he seemed younger when he laughed.

Suddenly the smile faded from her father's face. Emer looked behind her to see if something had happened, but she saw nothing out of the ordinary in the crowded theatre bar.

'What is it, Eamon?' asked Mam.

'Inspector Adams,' answered Dad.

Emer had heard her father discussing Inspector Adams, a Special Branch police officer based in Dublin Castle. He had once had an account at Smyths, the grocers where Dad had worked before going into business for himself, and they had known each other slightly back then. Now, however, he specialised in keeping track of nationalist activity, and Emer felt a sudden flutter of butterflies in her tummy.

She looked around again and saw a ramrod-straight man in a dress suit approaching. He had close-cropped grey hair and carried himself with a military bearing, and Emer knew without being told that he was Inspector Adams. He didn't look like the kind of man who would attend a pantomime for entertainment, and the horrible thought entered Emer's mind that maybe he was here to make an arrest.

But surely if he was going to detain Dad for his activities in the Volunteers, he would do it at home or when he was out drilling? Unless maybe he had a nasty streak and wanted to humiliate Dad by arresting him in front of everybody. Emer felt her stomach tighten, but she tried to convince herself that the approaching man was here with his wife, or perhaps treating a favourite niece or nephew to the pantomime.

And besides, if he wanted to arrest someone prominent, there were more senior figures than Dad – men like James Connolly of the Irish Citizen Army, or Padraig Pearse, who hadn't been arrested despite making a very inflammatory political speech at the graveside of the nationalist Jeremiah O'Donovan Rossa.

Emer looked back at her father, trying to gauge his reaction to seeing the policeman. He didn't actually look frightened, but all the fun had gone out of him and he seemed on guard. Emer noticed that Mam had placed her hand on his arm, and she wasn't sure if it was to reassure Dad or to restrain him.

Suddenly Emer felt scared. If this man were to take away her father, what would she and Mam do? She glanced around again and saw that the policeman was much nearer. He looked at her father, who held his gaze, and Emer found herself holding her breath. Then Inspector Adams gave a curt nod of recognition, Dad nodded back, and the man continued on his way.

Emer breathed out, hugely relieved. Mam and Dad began chatting again as if everything was normal, but Emer sensed that they were doing it for her benefit. She thought that while this time everything was fine, in future it might not be, if matters came to a head between the government and the Volunteers.

Just then the drinks arrived, and Emer smiled at her parents and sipped her lemonade. But although the drink tasted delicious, and the second act was still to come, things had changed. Emer sensed that no matter how they tried to disguise it, from now on they would always be looking over their shoulders.

Jack loved his family's annual New Year's Eve party – or 'hooley', as Ma always called it – and he sang along with everyone else in the living room as Da performed his party piece, 'In the Good Old Summertime'.

Da often invited younger members of the force who didn't have relations in Dublin to the party, and now the clean-cut young constables joined in singing with the family and their neighbours and friends. Ma served plates of Irish stew, and there were mince pies, Christmas cake and pudding on the table, while whiskey, porter, sherry and lemonade were all in ready supply. As usual the party was lively, but the presence of the policemen from Da's station brought Jack's mind back to the incident in Monasterevin and the difficult decision he had had to make.

He had sneaked back to bed that night without waking Ben, then wrestled with his conscience. He thought of what Phelim O'Connell had said about accepting that people could be on opposing sides and agreeing to differ. That same week the British Army had abandoned their disastrous campaign in Gallipoli, and Jack reasoned that, compared to the huge waste of life in the

Dardanelles, a few cases of explosives weren't all that significant.

The strongest argument of all, though, was Emer's point: the Irish Volunteers needed arms to counter-balance the huge number of weapons that the loyalist Ulster Volunteer Force had imported. And so, finally, Jack had decided that if the government could ignore the UVF importing weapons, then he could ignore the Volunteers doing the same thing on a much smaller scale.

Jack believed that he had done the right thing, yet part of him felt slightly guilty now as he watched Da singing. Once more he was keeping a secret from his father, who had been more understanding than many a parent would have been about the fight with Phelim. Still, he had made his decision, and what Da didn't know needn't worry him. His father finished his song to much applause, then Ma pointed at the clock.

'It's almost twelve, John. Countdown time!'

Jack watched as his father took his fob watch from his waistcoat pocket and consulted it. It was a long-standing tradition that Da counted off the final seconds of the year, and everybody joined him in the chant: 'Ten, nine, eight, seven, six, five, four, three, two, one – Happy New Year!'

It was now 1916. Everyone cheered, and Jack was hugged by Ma, Da and each of his four sisters. Bells across the city began to chime. Da led a chorus of 'Auld Lang Syne' and the party-goers sang, their arms intertwined. Jack could never understand what the words of the song meant, but he sang along happily. They followed another tradition and opened the hall door, letting everyone spill out onto the street.

Many of the other neighbours had done the same, and the cool night air was alive with exchanged greetings, ringing church bells and the distant sound of ships' horns from the docks.

Jack waved across the street to Joan, and soon he would go around the corner to see Ben and Gladys on Glenard Avenue. Emer and Mr and Mrs Davey had gone to a party in Rathmines, and while Jack would have liked to greet Emer, in another way he was relieved. With Mr Davey involved with the Volunteers, and with so many policemen here outside Jack's house, the Daveys' presence might have been a little awkward for everyone.

Jack stood on the pavement outside his home, his mind going back over the past year. He had nearly drowned, he had encountered armed men up in the mountains, he had fought Phelim O'Connell and then made peace with him, he had swum in the gala and he had seen dynamite being smuggled in Monasterevin. It had been an exciting year but also a sad one, in which his cousin had lost his leg and thousands of soldiers had died at the Western Front, in the Dardanelles and in other theatres of war.

Jack hoped that 1916 would be a better year. And he hoped that Da and Mr Davey wouldn't be in conflict. Still, there was nothing that he could do about any of that now. And so he banished his worries and started up the road, eager to see Ben and Gladys and to wish them luck for whatever the new year might bring.

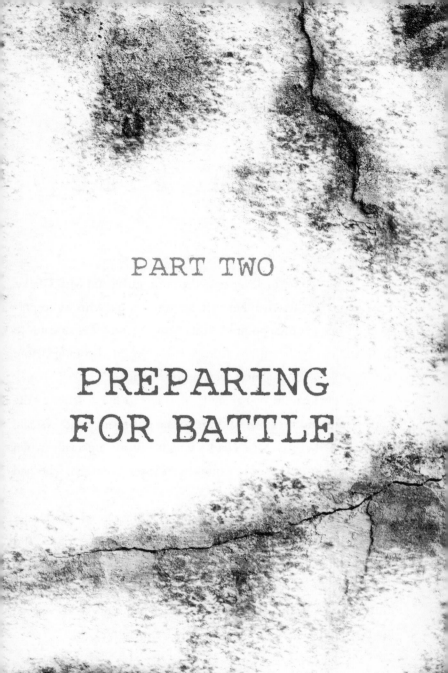

PART TWO

PREPARING
FOR BATTLE

CHAPTER SEVENTEEN

APRIL 1916

'**N**othing ever stays the same, girls!' said Miss Clarke. 'Remember that, because people who try to prevent change get disappointed. And history isn't a series of dates to be learnt off by heart. No, history is the world changing before our eyes, sometimes almost without our noticing.'

Emer sat forward in her desk, listening to her teacher as the spring sunshine streamed in through the classroom windows. She revelled in the way Miss Clarke taught history, especially when compared with the boring approach of Sister Assumpta, who had taken the previous class.

Today was Spy Wednesday – a name that Emer loved – and Sister Assumpta had given the girls a really dull Easter talk about Judas and his betrayal of Jesus to the Pharisees. Emer had wondered what made Judas do it, which was the kind of thing that Miss Clarke might have turned into a fascinating discussion. Sister Assumpta didn't engage in discussion, however, and had simply lectured the girls.

As if to illustrate their differing styles, Miss Clarke now asked the class, 'Who can give me an example of a recent change that in time will seem historic?'

'Women in Norway getting the vote, Miss?' said Joan.

'Excellent example. Anyone else?'

'The new rule that says women replacing men in factories must be paid the same rate as men?' suggested Emer.

'Interesting choice, Emer,' said Miss Clarke. 'But there's a condition, isn't there? They get equal pay *provided the work is of the same quality as was previously done by the men*. Does that seem fair to you, Emer?'

'Eh, yes, Miss, I suppose so.'

'And yet when only men did the work, some did it well, and others no doubt did it badly. But they all got paid the same. No-one thought to say that only men *doing quality work* should get the going rate. So while it *is* a historical development, maybe it's not quite as progressive as it seems.'

Emer loved the way Miss Clarke made you question things like this, and she watched with interest as Joan raised her hand again.

'Cancelling the Olympics until the war is over would count as historic, wouldn't it, Miss?' said Joan.

'Yes, I think so. Are you in favour of that, Joan?'

'Well, my dad says it's only right.'

'A view to which he's entitled. But what do *you* think, Joan?'

'Well … I suppose it wouldn't be fair on the soldiers to go

ahead without them. Not when they're suffering so much away at the front.'

Miss Clarke and the class discussed the merits of this, and Emer grew reflective. The front to which Joan referred was the Western Front in France and Belgium, but Emer feared that there might soon be a front right here in Dublin. Her father was scheduled for three days of manoeuvres over the Easter weekend, and Emer had picked up on hints from her parents' conversations that the Volunteers might be preparing for armed conflict. It was exhilarating to think of the Volunteers fighting for Irish freedom, but scary that Dad could get hurt – or even killed – in the process.

'Emer?' said Miss Clarke, bringing her out of her reverie. 'Are we boring you?'

'No, Miss.'

'You looked like you were miles away.'

'No, Miss, I'm really interested in what makes history,' she said. Then she put the Volunteers from her mind and sat up attentively.

'Who can tell me what a tercentenary is?' asked Brother McGill.

Jack looked in surprise at his desk mate, Gerry Quinn, who had raised his hand. Normally Gerry didn't shine during English class, but the school was breaking up for Easter holidays today so maybe he was feeling perkier than usual.

'Is it the third anniversary of something, Brother?' he said.

Brother McGill smiled condescendingly. 'I think, Mr Quinn, you know more about horses and carts than the English language!'

Some of the boys laughed, wanting to win favour with the teacher, but Jack didn't join in. Why couldn't Giller see that it was mean to belittle Gerry on one of the rare occasions when he put himself forward?

'Anyone else know?' asked the teacher.

Phelim O'Connell raised his hand. 'Is it the three-hundredth anniversary of something, Brother?'

'*Maith an fear*, Phelim!' said Brother McGill approvingly. '*Maith an fear*. And does anybody know *whose* tercentenary falls around now?'

Jack knew the answer, but he was still annoyed at Giller, so he didn't raise his hand. Although Gerry hadn't reacted outwardly to the brother's comments, Jack sensed that his feelings had been hurt. On the other hand Jack was aware that Gerry really disliked Phelim, so anything that undermined Phelim as teacher's pet would appeal to Gerry. Maybe he should answer before the other boy got a chance to shine again.

Jack raised his hand. 'Shakespeare, sir,' he said. 'He died three hundred years ago this week.'

'Shakespeare is right, Mr Madigan.' Brother McGill looked at his pupils and smirked. '"The Bard of Avon", as he's referred to on our neighbouring isle,' he added mockingly.

Jack didn't really like Shakespeare – he found his old-fashioned English hard to understand – but if Brother McGill wanted to be an Irish nationalist, why couldn't he just take pride in Irish writers, without mocking English playwrights like Shakespeare?

Jack couldn't risk antagonising his teacher by saying so, but recently he had felt more at one than ever before with the British Empire. His cousin Ronnie had been awarded a medal for the action in which he had lost his leg, and his uncle Bertie was still on active service with the British Army. These facts combined with the news of last month's Zeppelin air raids by the Germans, in which civilians had been killed, all made him root for an Allied victory and dislike the pettiness of Giller's nationalism.

The war itself, however, had become terrifying, the losses so crippling that the government had brought in conscription in England. So far it had been resisted in Ireland, but who could tell when that might change? Jack had read in the paper that two million more women were working in the United Kingdom than a year ago, so things could change very quickly, and Da's job as a policeman was no guarantee that he wouldn't be called up.

But Easter was coming, and on Good Friday he would go to church and do the Stations of the Cross. He would pray for a speedy end to the war. And if that wasn't possible, he would pray that Da wasn't conscripted, that Uncle Bertie stayed safe and that Ronnie continued to recover from his wounds. Buoyed by the thought, Jack gave Gerry a conspiratorial nod, then he pretended to be interested as Brother McGill continued the class.

CHAPTER EIGHTEEN

Emer's stomach was tight with tension, and her mouth felt dry. It was Easter Sunday night. Her mouth had felt dry earlier in the day too, when she had gorged on chocolate Easter eggs. Now, though, one part of her was excited and another part frightened as she listened to her father, his voice unusually serious as he gave Mam a series of instructions.

Her parents were talking in the kitchen, but the door was ajar. Emer was eavesdropping unashamedly in the hall, rooted to the spot by her father's revelations.

It seemed that the Volunteers' three days of manoeuvres were a ruse to fool the British authorities, and an armed uprising was going to take place tomorrow. Dad had explained that it was originally planned for today but had been postponed until tomorrow morning.

Dad had withdrawn a large sum of money from the bank, on the basis that there might be chaos in the aftermath of an uprising. Now he was giving Mam instructions about closing their two grocery shops for the coming week but paying the staff their wages.

'How soon will we re-open, Eamon?' asked Mam, her voice strained.

'We can review it after a week. If I'm still in action, or taken prisoner, it will be your decision. But if the city is in chaos, stay closed until things calm down.'

'Right.'

'And if anything, err on the side of caution.'

'But you won't be doing that, will you?' retorted Mam.

'Come on, Molly,' replied Dad gently. 'Once I joined the Volunteers, we knew this day would come.'

'I know. But don't … don't make a point of being a hero.'

Emer could hear the fear in her mother's words. She felt frightened herself on Dad's behalf, but his next words shocked her.

'These are the tickets,' he said to Mam. 'I booked yourself and Emer on tomorrow's twelve o'clock train to Ennis.'

No! thought Emer. *There's going to be a revolution in Dublin. I can't miss out on it!*

'Dad!' she said, suddenly opening the door and entering the kitchen. 'I couldn't help overhearing.' That wasn't strictly true, but it was no time for splitting hairs. 'Please, don't send me away. This is history happening. Mam and I will be safe here. Please don't send us out of Dublin!'

Dad looked at her, his face deeply serious. 'What I told Mam is top secret, Emer. Absolutely top secret. Lots of Volunteers know nothing about what we're going to do tomorrow. Do you understand that?'

'Yes, Dad.'

'Be sure you do. And as for staying here, that's out of the question.'

'But, Dad—'

'No buts! Civilians get killed in wars all the time, Emer.'

'The war won't be on our street.'

'It could spread all over the city. Artillery or machine-gun fire doesn't distinguish between soldiers and civilians. And even if there's no fighting round here, maybe they'll raid the homes of Volunteer officers. Maybe they'll arrest family members.'

Emer hadn't thought of that, and she struggled for an answer.

'It's for the best, pet,' said Mam. 'I don't want to stay away from Dublin when Dad's in danger. But it's better for Dad, and for us, if he knows we're safe in Ennis with Aunt May.'

'You want to play your part, Emer, don't you?' asked Dad.

'Yes.'

'Then free me. Free me to fight for Ireland without having to worry about my family. Will you do that, Emer?'

She looked at her father, and with every fibre of her being she hated what he was asking of her. She imagined herself when she was old and her grandchildren queried what she did in the uprising of 1916. *'Oh, I missed that. I left Dublin the day it started and stayed down in Ennis!'*

'Emer? Will you do that for me?' Her father's eyes bored into her, and she found it impossible to defy him.

'OK,' she said.

'Good girl,' answered Dad. 'And like I said – not the faintest hint of this to a living soul. Not to *anyone*. All right?'

'Right,' said Emer, and she nodded in agreement. She was

still frustrated at being sidelined but excited at the idea of the coming revolution.

Jack tossed and turned in his bed, unable to sleep. Even though he loved music, he hated the way a song sometimes went round and round in his head. His sister Mary had earned a lot of overtime at the munitions factory this week, and from her pay she had bought a gramophone record of the song 'Down at the Old Bull and Bush'. Now its catchy melody played maddeningly in his head and wouldn't allow Jack to drift off to sleep.

It had been an eventful day. Jack had gone to Mass for Easter Sunday with his family, then played football on the street, before dropping over to Gerry Quinn with a small Easter egg. Jack knew that Gerry's uncle might not buy him any eggs, and Ma had suggested giving one to Gerry from the collection that Jack and his sisters had accumulated. Gerry had been grateful, and Jack had happily accepted in return a somewhat battered Hotspur annual as an Easter present, knowing that the gesture made Gerry feel more of an equal.

Jack had returned home for a big Easter Sunday dinner – a long-standing family tradition – at which Da made a toast and Ma gave thanks for their good fortune, offering up a prayer for Uncle Bertie's safe-keeping and cousin Ronnie's continued recovery from his amputation.

The war was still raging bloodily in Europe, however, and just two days ago the Royal Navy had successfully intercepted a ship off the coast of Kerry that was carrying arms for the Volunteers. The thought of the Volunteers made Jack's racing mind shift to Emer. Soon they would be swimming again in the Tolka. He was grateful to her for the huge improvements he had made as a swimmer, and for being such a great friend. But while swimming in the river was something to look forward to, Emer's father was a real source of worry to Jack. Lately Mr Davey had been very active with the Volunteers, and even though the Navy had prevented the recent shipment of arms from reaching them, the Volunteers had other weapons.

What would happen to Da – and other members of the unarmed DMP – if Mr Davey and the Volunteers decided to fight? It was a scary thought, and Jack struggled to dismiss it.

He shut his eyes tight and shifted to his other side, hoping that sleep would come and banish his fears.

CHAPTER NINETEEN

Emer tried not to arouse her mother's suspicions. What she was about to do would be the most daring act of her life, but she had to control her excitement and make Mam think that she was behaving normally. They were sitting together in the carriage of the twelve o'clock train that would take them from Dublin's Kingsbridge Station to the safety of Ennis in County Clare.

The train was due to pull out any moment now, but Emer forced herself to sit still and not act too hastily. For her ruse to work she had to time things perfectly, and she hoped that she could pull off the required deceit.

She had decided last night that no matter what her parents said, she *had* to be in Dublin for the uprising. She made her plans accordingly but pretended to go along with the trip to Ennis. This morning Dad had gone to join his fellow rebels, and she and Mam had bade him a tearful goodbye, their fear for his well-being mingled with huge pride in his playing an active role in the rebellion.

Now Emer glanced out the carriage window at the station clock. One minute to go. She breathed out slowly to try to calm herself, and Mam looked enquiringly at her. 'Are you all right, pet?'

'Yes, Mam,' she answered, striving to keep her voice normal. 'Just … just excited for Dad, but nervous too.' This was true, so it made sense to let Mam think that any nervousness stemmed from this.

'I'm sure Dad will be fine,' said Mam in a low voice that the other passengers couldn't hear. 'I've trusted him to Our Lady's care, and we'll both pray for him.'

Emer wasn't as religious as her mother, but she nodded in agreement. 'I'll pray for him every day.'

Emer glanced out the window again, willing the clock onwards, but the seconds passed with frustrating slowness. A train guard moved along the platform with a green flag in his hand, and Emer realised that the time had come. She rose as casually as she could. 'I'm going down to the toilet, Mam. Back in a while.'

'All right, love.'

Emer felt a sudden stab of guilt, and on the spur of the moment she reached out and squeezed her mother's arm.

Mam looked at her in mild surprise, but Emer forced herself to give a reassuring smile, then turned away and walked briskly along the aisle. She heard the slamming of carriage doors as the station staff began preparing for the train's departure, and she realised that she needed to move quickly to deal with the conductor, whom she saw at the end of the next carriage. Reaching into her pocket, she withdrew a shilling coin and an envelope containing the letter she had written this morning. She had thought about what to write for a long time, but in the end she had kept it really simple.

Sorry to trick you, Mam, but today is a huge day in
Irish history, and I have to stay and see it. Please, please
don't come back to Dublin for me – I won't be staying
at home, so there's absolutely no point. But I will stay
safe, and I promise to write to put your mind at ease
and to tell you what I know about how Dad is doing.
Please don't be too cross with me, I just had to do this.

Your loving daughter,

Emer

Emer approached the conductor and handed him the letter.
He was a gaunt, hungry-looking man, and as she had hoped, he
instinctively reached out and took it. 'Please deliver this for me,'
she said. 'Two carriages up, the lady in seat twelve. She's wearing a
green dress and a fawn hat.'

The man looked at her in surprise, and Emer spoke quickly,
wanting to get off the train before it pulled away. 'It's really important that you don't give it to her for fifteen minutes.'

'Look, I don't know–'

'I'll give you a shilling,' said Emer, cutting the man short. It was
two weeks' pocket money for Emer, and even for an adult worker
like the conductor, it would be a significant sum. 'Please. All you
have to do is wait fifteen minutes and then hand it to her.'

Emer heard a whistle and she knew the train was about to pull off.

'What are you up to?' said the man.

'I have to leave. Please. Just give her the letter. Have we a deal?'

Emer heard a release of steam, then the train shuddered and she knew it was about to move off. 'Come on, you'll never make an easier shilling!' she urged.

The man hesitated for another second, then suddenly took the money.

'All right,' he said.

'Seat twelve – and wait fifteen minutes!' said Emer, then she quickly turned to the carriage door and pulled down the handle. The door swung open, and Emer jumped down onto the platform just as the train began to move off.

'What the hell are you at?' cried the guard on the platform.

'Sorry, change of plan!' answered Emer, then she reached forward and slammed the door shut as the train began to move away.

The guard looked like he was about to protest, but Emer pointed behind him towards the engine. 'I think he wants you!' she cried.

The guard turned around, and while he was distracted Emer ran down the platform, then lost herself in the crowds milling about the station. Her heart was thumping, and she knew that eventually she would be in enormous trouble with her parents – but she didn't care. Revolution was in the air, and she wasn't going to miss out on it. Moving through the smoke-scented station, she made for the exit, then she stepped out into the bright sunshine and headed for the city centre, eager for her adventure to begin.

'Have you heard?' asked Joan, her eyes wide with excitement.

Jack and Ben had been playing with Ben's cricket bat and a tennis ball at the sunlit corner of Ellesmere Avenue when their friend ran up to them. 'Heard what?' Jack said.

'There's been a rebellion! The Volunteers have occupied places all over the city!'

'No!' exclaimed Ben.

'Yes,' answered Joan. 'They've signed a proclamation declaring a republic, and taken the GPO and the Four Courts, and they're fighting the army!'

Jack was horrified. Even though the Volunteers had been manoeuvring a lot lately, this was a shock.

'That's awful!' said Ben. 'The army are fighting the Germans, and now they get attacked at home!'

'I wonder is Mr Davey involved,' said Joan.

'He could be,' answered Ben. 'Maybe that's why Emer and Mrs Davey went down the country. What do you think, Jack?'

'I think this is a disaster,' said Jack quietly. 'A total disaster.' Because he knew it wasn't the army that kept law and order in the first place – it was the police. And Da had reported for duty to his police station in Kilmainham early this morning. *An unarmed policeman in a city that is suddenly at war*, thought Jack with growing unease.

'I'd say the army will put manners on them in jig time,' said Ben.

'I wouldn't be so sure,' said Joan. 'It sounds like they've taken everyone by surprise, including the army.'

'Did you hear anything about the police?' asked Jack.

'No,' said Joan. 'Is your dad on duty?'

Jack nodded.

'I'm sure he'll be fine. They're hardly going to shoot other Irishmen.'

Jack hoped she was right. But despite the sunny weather, he felt a chill running up his spine.

'Don't you dare laugh at me!' said Emer. 'I'm Eamon Davey's daughter, and he's out risking his life today!'

She had gone to a barricade at North King Street to offer to be a runner for the rebels. Emer had chosen the location carefully, having spent the last few hours experiencing the exciting chaos that was Dublin city centre. She had discovered that the Volunteers and the Irish Citizen Army had joined forces, with the rebel leaders Padraig Pearse and James Connolly setting up headquarters in the GPO. She had heard that her father was liaising for the Volunteers with the Citizen Army unit sent to occupy either Dublin Castle or City Hall – there was confusion about which. Emer chose the barricade at North King Street because it was far enough from her father not to bump into him, but near enough that she might hear how he was faring.

It was also a good location in that the area between here and the GPO was familiar to her from visits to the fruit and vegetable markets with Dad. But the men on the barricade had laughingly dismissed her offer of assistance, and so Emer had snapped at them. The women of Cumann na mBan were fighting in the Rising, and the boys of the Fianna movement, so why shouldn't she play a part also? The men seemed taken aback by her outburst, and she realised that Dad's name had bought her credibility.

'Are you really Eamon Davey's daughter?' asked an older Volunteer who seemed to have more authority than his comrades.

'Yes, I am,' answered Emer.

The man stared at her, then nodded. 'You've obviously inherited your da's pluck as well as his looks.'

'Thank you. Have you heard anything about his unit?'

'They couldn't take Dublin Castle. But they've occupied City Hall.'

Emer was thrilled that her father was involved in such important operations, but she also felt scared for him. 'Have there … have there been casualties?' she asked.

'I don't know,' answered the man. 'And really, you should get home before you become a casualty yourself.'

'No,' answered Emer, 'I should help out. Look, it's only a matter of time before the British get reinforcements. When that happens you're going to need every single man you have. Let me run your reports to headquarters; it will free up a fighter to man the barricades here.'

Emer could see that the Volunteer was half persuaded, so she pressed on. 'I've a better chance of not being stopped than an adult. If you jot down a quick report now, I could get it to the GPO. Please. You know it makes sense.'

The man considered this for a moment, then took a sheet of paper from his pocket, quickly wrote a note and handed it to Emer. 'OK, get that to Commander Pearse.'

'I will.'

'And Emer?'

'Yes?'

'It's only a report. It's not worth getting killed for. If it's too dangerous getting to Sackville Street, turn back. All right?'

'Right,' said Emer. But this was her first mission, and she had no intention of turning back.

'Good girl,' said the Volunteer. 'Up the Republic!'

'Up the Republic!' answered Emer, then she slipped the note into her cardigan pocket, turned around and headed towards the centre of town.

'Please, Ma, let me go to Kilmainham!'

Jack and his mother were in the sun-warmed kitchen. Ma was organising dinner, in what he sensed was a vain attempt at keeping things normal.

'No, love,' she answered, 'that's out of the question.'

'But I could cycle over to the station in half an hour, and then we'd know if Da was OK.'

'The city's in chaos, Jack! Bad enough that Da and the girls are out. I'm not having you at risk too!'

Jack's sisters had gone to the races at Fairyhouse in County Meath, and there was no telling when they might return to the unexpectedly war-torn city.

'Da will contact us when he can,' said Ma.

'Yes, but–'

'Jack!' said Ma, cutting him off. 'Da wouldn't want you risking yourself out on the streets. And neither do I, so that's an end to it.'

'OK,' answered Jack reluctantly. With the city in uproar – and it seemed now that the rebels had seized buildings all over Dublin – it made sense that Da hadn't been able to get home or send word to reassure them. But even though Ma refused to say it, there was another possible explanation: Da could be injured. Or even worse. *No!* thought Jack. *I have to stay positive.* But war was unpredictable, and he wished with all his heart that he could be sure his father was all right.

Emer felt a bullet whistling past her ear as she sprinted for the corner of Halston Street. It had taken all of her nerve to escape from the British soldiers after they stopped her and found the report she was bringing to rebel headquarters. She had run down Cuckoo Lane, zigzagging to put the soldiers off their aim, but the volley of shots they unleashed had been terrifyingly loud, and some of the ricocheting bullets had hit the cobblestones near her feet.

She ducked low now, still zigzagging, and ignored her pounding chest as she tried desperately to up her speed. The corner was just ahead, yet it seemed to take forever to reach it. Another deafening series of shots rang out just as Emer reached the junction.

She flinched, half expecting the pain of a bullet in the back, then suddenly she was safely round the corner. She saw Halston Street Church on her left and ran in through the entrance gates. Still moving at speed, Emer almost collided with an old lady who was coming out. She quickly apologised, then swung open the porch door and entered the church proper. It was darker in here, and the air smelt of incense and wax from the candles that were burning at a small side altar.

At this hour of the afternoon there was nobody else in the church. Emer moved quickly up the aisle, seeking a hiding place. Her best hope was that the soldiers would continue down Halston Street and eventually conclude that they had lost her in one of the side streets. But equally they might follow her into the church, deciding that its open door made it a likely destination.

Emer scanned the church, her mind racing. There was a door at the side of the altar – maybe it would lead to another part of the building where she could hide. But if she went in there, she might run into a sacristan or one of the priests. She looked around frantically, knowing that if the soldiers followed her into the church, they would be here soon. She saw a row of confession boxes, and acting on instinct, she ran to the furthest one, quickly pulled open the door and entered the darkened interior.

She fell to her knees, keeping her head below the grille on the door that allowed a small amount of light into the gloom of the confessional. No sooner had she settled herself than she heard the sound of the porch door closing. *Someone else was here.* Emer held her breath as she listened to their heavy footsteps. She knew at once that they weren't made by the shoes of the elderly women and men who frequented churches on sunny afternoons. *Army boots*, thought Emer.

She kept absolutely still as the steps drew nearer. Barely daring to breathe, Emer listened as the person went past her. Suddenly the footsteps stopped. Was he looking around the church now, scanning it for hiding places? And if so, were the confessionals an obvious place to search? Just then Emer heard the sound of the porch door closing again and another set of footsteps.

'No sign of her, Corp,' said this second man. 'Must have scarpered down a side street.'

'Damn her!'

Emer recognised with dread the voice of the scary corporal who had questioned her and found the note.

'Bad luck to swear in church, Corp,' said the second man.

'Don't talk rubbish!'

'Sorry, I just–'

'And she mightn't have scarpered at all. She could be in this building.'

'Is she really worth finding, Corp? She's only a runner, and we took her message. And Alf's still bleeding. Should we not just leave it and get him to a medic?'

Emer prayed that the corporal would follow the other soldier's suggestion. There was a pause, then the first man spoke: 'Little Shinner bitch, I'd like to lay my hands on her! But yeah, better look after Alf.'

The two men quickly walked off, and Emer allowed herself to breathe out. After a moment she heard the porch door closing, and she felt a flood of relief. This had been the most frightening experience of her life, but she felt exhilarated at having come through it. Not that she was in the clear yet. She still had to risk getting to the GPO so that she could deliver verbally the message from the Volunteers at North King Street. Luckily her curiosity had got the better of her earlier, and she had read the note before the patrol had intercepted her. She could still pass on the report and explain that the British now knew its contents.

She remained kneeling in the confession box, giving the soldiers plenty of time to be on their way. Gradually her breathing returned to normal, and she told herself that it was time to move on. Gathering her courage, she left the church, stepped out again into the bright sunlight and continued with her mission.

'Two policemen have been shot dead!'

Jack felt as though an icy hand had clutched his heart. He wanted to speak, but the words wouldn't come out. His sisters had finally managed to get home from the races at Fairyhouse, and Maureen was pale-faced as she led the others into the kitchen to deliver this awful news.

'Oh my God!' said Ma.

'Have … have they said who they are?' asked Jack. His fear must have shown on his face, because Maureen reached out and squeezed his arm.

'Da's not one of them.'

Jack felt enormously relieved, though of course it was dreadful that any policeman should be shot dead.

'Who were they?' asked Ma.

'One was called James O'Brien. The other was a Michael Lahiff – he was on duty at Stephen's Green.'

'I don't know either of them,' said Ma. 'But it's cold-blooded murder, shooting unarmed men.'

'There's another rumour that the rebels captured a policeman at the GPO and they're holding him prisoner,' said Sheila.

'Rumours are flying all over the place,' added Mary. 'They're saying the DMP are being ordered off the streets before any more get shot.'

'Proper order,' said Ma.

'So that could explain why Da hasn't come home,' suggested Mary, 'if they've all been ordered back to barracks.'

Jack wanted to believe this, but if policemen were being shot and taken prisoner, that could have happened to Da too. 'I still think I should cycle over to Kilmainham,' he said. 'I could be there and back in an hour, and if Da is up to his eyes in the station, then at least we'd know he's OK.'

'Nobody leaves this house for Kilmainham!' said Ma firmly. 'Da is well able to look after himself. But the city's gone mad, so he's probably run off his feet. He'll be back to us as soon as he can, and that's an end to it.'

Ma spoke with conviction, but Jack sensed that she was putting on a brave face. Yes, his father was strong and brave and able to look after himself, but what good was that if he was unarmed and someone tried to shoot him? He couldn't bear to think of anything happening to Da, and he desperately wanted to know if he was safe. He would obey Ma for now, he decided. But if Da hadn't returned home by tomorrow morning, then he was going to go looking for him.

Emer hid behind the trees and watched as Gerry Quinn's uncle cracked his whip, then pulled away in his horse and cart from the cottage at the Tolka. Emer stood unmoving until the cart passed out of sight. Satisfied that she hadn't been seen, she stepped out wearily and made for the doorway of Gerry's home in the fading evening light.

The darkening sky was a deep shade of blue, but Emer was oblivious to its beauty after a momentous but exhausting day. She had managed to deliver the message to the rebel headquarters at the GPO, but then she had been ordered to stand down as a runner. Emer had tried to argue, but a Volunteer officer had insisted that twelve-year-old girls were not combatants. He said that she was being given a direct military order, the disobeying of which would be mutiny.

Emer had turned away unhappily. She was frustrated that her time as a runner had ended, yet if she were honest, a tiny part of her was also relieved that she wouldn't have to face the consequences of being caught again. And so she had tramped her way around the chaos of the city centre before eventually heading for the banks of the Tolka, where she waited until she could be sure of talking to Gerry without his uncle being present.

She approached the door now, and she could see that an oil lamp was burning inside the cottage. She had no idea how Gerry would react to what she was going to ask him, and she paused briefly to get up her nerve, then reached out and knocked on the door. After a moment it opened, and she saw the surprise on Gerry's face.

'Emer. What are you doing here?'

'I'm ... I'm looking for help.' She saw that Gerry looked puzzled, and she opened her hands in appeal. 'I know ... I know we aren't close friends, but I've no-one else to turn to.'

'For what?'

'Somewhere to stay the night. My Dad's part of the uprising, and Volunteers' families might be rounded up. Our home could be raided, so I can't stay there.'

'Why didn't you ask Gladys or Joan?'

'They live near to our house, so I might be traced to them.'

'But no-one would think of you staying in a shack like this?'

'That's ... that's not what I meant.'

'But that's how it is.'

Emer felt uncomfortable. 'Look, I'm sorry if—'

'It's OK,' he said, cutting her off. 'You're right, they won't think of here. So come in, you can stay.'

'Thanks, Gerry. I'm really grateful,' said Emer, stepping in through the doorway and following him into a sparsely furnished kitchen. There was a smell of food, and Emer realised just how hungry she was.

Gerry must have seen her gazing at the pot of food on the stove. 'Rabbit stew,' he said. 'I caught one this morning.'

'Really?'

'Yeah. Have you ever had rabbit stew?'

'No, actually. But it smells delicious.'

'Are you hungry?'

'Well ... yes, a bit, but I don't want to—'

'Sit down. I'll get you a bowl.'

'Are you sure?'

'Yeah, you're grand.'

As Gerry organised the food and cutlery, Emer looked at the

battered furnishings and realised that this was the poorest house she had ever been in. And yet Gerry was not just putting her up but also sharing his stew. Emer was touched that someone who had so little would be so generous. She suddenly felt emotional, and she turned away so Gerry wouldn't notice her becoming teary-eyed.

'Here you go,' he said, ladling the stew into a bowl and placing it on the table.

'Thanks.' Emer had surreptitiously wiped her eyes, and now she took up a spoon and began eating the food. 'It's gorgeous,' she said.

'Yeah, it's one of the few things Uncle Pat is good at cooking.'

'Will it be OK with him that I stay here?'

Gerry shook his head. 'Better he doesn't know. You take my bed, and I'll kip on the bedroom floor on some cushions.'

'That's really kind. But will your uncle not come into the room to say goodnight?'

'No, he never does that.'

Emer resumed eating the stew. She thought that Gerry's answer was really sad, but before she could think of a response, he continued. 'He's gone out drinking now, so he'll fall into bed when he gets back and sleep it off in the morning.'

'Yeah?'

'I seen him do it loads of times. You'll be fine.'

'I don't know how to thank you.'

'No point trying then,' said Gerry with a wry grin. He looked at her curiously. 'You never said where your ma is staying.'

'Ennis, in County Clare. I was supposed to go there with her, but I hopped off the train without telling her.'

'Yeah? I'd say you'll be killed.'

'I just had to do it. And anyway, I'm more worried for Dad than about what Mam will say.'

'Do you know where your father is fighting?'

'It could be Dublin Castle, it could be City Hall.'

'Right.'

'I'm dead proud of him, Gerry. But I'm really scared that he'll be hurt.'

'Well, loads of people are going to be hurt.'

Emer had been hoping for words of consolation, but instead Gerry had spoken truthfully.

'No use fretting about that now, though,' he added. 'So eat up, get a good night's sleep and worry about tomorrow when it comes. That's what I do.'

'Yeah,' said Emer. Then she returned to the food and tried to put from her mind the horror of what could happen to her father.

CHAPTER TWENTY

Jack sped down the hill on his bicycle. The Phoenix Park was fresh and green in its spring foliage, and the sweet-smelling air swept his hair back as he rose in the saddle and accelerated down the incline.

It was Tuesday morning now, and he was making for Kilmainham to try to find out what had happened to Da. Although his mother had expressly forbidden such a journey, there had been no word from his father, and Jack couldn't take the uncertainty any longer. Ma would be frantic with worry if she knew what he was doing, so he had quietly sneaked his bike out and told only Mary where he was going. Mary had tried to dissuade him, but Jack insisted that for everyone's sake they had to enquire about Da. He warned Mary not to tell Ma about his expedition unless it was absolutely necessary.

It felt good to be doing something at last, but the closer he got to Kilmainham, the more worried Jack was about Da's absence. He could hear gunfire in the distance, and the city was rife with rumours of killings and general mayhem. There was talk of artillery being brought to bear on the rebel strongholds. Neither Dublin Port nor the city's two main railway stations were in rebel hands, and British Army reinforcements were said to be on their way. The Volunteers and the Citizen Army had chosen strategic locations, however, and were laying down gunfire to prevent easy access of more troops into the city. Jack had avoided the quays near Kingsbridge Station, taking the safer route to Kilmainham through the Phoenix Park.

He turned left at the base of the Magazine Hill, then exited the park and made for Islandbridge. Looking back towards town, he could see thick smoke rising into the blue April sky, and the sound of machine-gun fire carried on the breeze. And this was just a day after the uprising had begun. What sort of slaughter would take place if thousands of troops poured into the city — and if they began using artillery? Jack tried to dismiss his negative thoughts and told himself that whatever happened, Da would come through. He rose into the saddle again and cycled hard up the slope towards Kilmainham.

'My God, Gerry!' said Emer. 'What have you done?' She had stepped from the bedroom of the cottage into the kitchen and now stood in shock, looking at the goods on the cracked wooden table.

Exhaustion had set in the previous night, and she had slept soundly despite the strange surroundings of Gerry's bedroom. Then a few minutes ago she had been woken by Gerry's uncle clattering off in the horse and cart. His absence meant she could enter the sunlit kitchen, where she saw all the food and clothing spread out on the table, still in their shop wrappers.

Gerry didn't seem perturbed by her question. 'I done what everyone was doin'. I helped myself.'

Emer was taken aback, and despite her gratitude to Gerry for letting her stay overnight, she couldn't keep the disapproval from her voice. 'You were looting?'

'I went into town this morning. Other people were helping themselves, why shouldn't I?'

'But … but what about the shopkeepers?'

'They've been rich all their lives. With their big stores and their fancy clothes and more food than they can eat. This was a chance for poor people to come out on top, just for once.'

Emer could understand Gerry thinking like this, but she still felt uncomfortable with the idea of looting. 'You could have been arrested,' she said.

'No chance,' answered Gerry. 'The DMP have been pulled back to their barracks.'

'Why?'

'The rebels shot a few of them, so they're off the streets.'

'Really? Gosh, I hope Mr Madigan is all right.'

'Yeah. I don't like the peelers, but Jack's da sounds decent enough.'

'So what's it like in town?' asked Emer.

'Mad. The rebels have taken Boland's Mills, Stephen's Green, the South Dublin Union, Jacob's factory, the Four Courts and loads of other places.'

'Did you hear anything about Dublin Castle or City Hall?'

'They say the rebels never took Dublin Castle, and the army's taken back City Hall.'

Emer felt her stomach tighten. 'I really hope Dad's OK,' she said.

'He might have escaped. Or he could just be taken prisoner. You could always go down there and check it out.'

Emer considered this.

'Forget the police,' continued Gerry. 'They're cooped up in their barracks, so you needn't worry about them raiding your house or stopping you in the street.'

Emer suspected that Gerry was right, and that both the police and the army had too much to contend with now to be raiding the houses of Volunteers. It meant that she could move back to her own home, but it still left the worry of her father.

'Want my advice?' asked Gerry.

'Yes.'

'Your clothes have got a bit messed up since yesterday. Go home and change into your best outfit, then go to City Hall and ask about your da.'

'Why my best outfit?'

''Cause if you look posh, officers and people in charge take you seriously.'

Emer hadn't thought of that before, but it was probably true.

'Whatever has happened your da, has happened to him. Right?'

Emer didn't want to think like that, but she nodded in reply.

'So you might as well be smart about it,' said Gerry. 'Have a bit of breakfast, then go home and freshen up. Change into your best clothes and go and ask the officer in charge at City Hall about your father. OK?'

'OK …' said Emer haltingly. 'OK.'

'I'm sorry, Jack, but I've bad news.' The policeman on duty at the desk was a colleague of Jack's father's called Sergeant Kirwan, whom he had met several times, and the man looked uneasy. The DMP barracks was bustling with activity: officers were barricading the windows with sandbags as reports came in of looting and rebel activity all over the city.

Jack was oblivious to everything around him as the man's words struck home. He dreaded to hear the worst but forced himself to ask. 'What's happened?'

'Your father … your father is missing.'

'Missing?'

'He's not on any casualty list, that's the good part.'

Jack felt a sense of relief, but it didn't last long; this could still mean that his dad was dead, with his body not yet found. 'When was he last seen?' he asked.

'Yesterday afternoon. It's possible … he may well have been taken prisoner.'

'Why would they want to hold a policeman prisoner?'

'He could have tried to stop them doing something. We've a definite report of an officer being held prisoner in the GPO.'

The sergeant reached out and laid a large hand reassuringly on Jack's shoulder. 'If he's a prisoner, he'll be all right.'

'How will he be? Haven't two DMP men been shot dead – even though the rebels know they're unarmed?'

The policeman didn't answer, and Jack saw that he was unshaven and his eyes looked bloodshot.

'That's true, son,' he said now. 'But from what we hear, most of the rebels are behaving honourably.'

'Could they win?'

The policeman shook his head at once. 'Not a chance. In a few days they'll be outnumbered ten to one. And they've no artillery, no heavy weapons. It's a hopeless cause.'

'If Da was taken prisoner, where could he be held?'

'Any of the rebel garrisons, I suppose.'

'Where's the most likely?'

'Well, the nearest fighting to here is the workhouse complex at the South Dublin Union. It's a huge place, and fierce battles are going on there – so he could be somewhere in the Union.'

'And when will the army retake it?'

'Impossible to tell. It's turmoil out there.'

'You have our address, Sergeant,' said Jack. 'Please, promise me the minute you hear anything, you'll tell us?'

'You have my word, Jack.'

'Thank you.'

'And keep your chin up. God is good.'

Jack thought this was a silly thing to say less than twenty-four hours after two unarmed policemen had been shot. He said nothing in reply but nodded in farewell, then made his way for the door, more worried than at any time since the Rising had begun.

'Excuse me, sir!' said Emer, trying to make her voice sound assured as she addressed the officer supervising the British troops strengthening the barricades at City Hall.

Earlier in the day Emer had taken Gerry's advice and gone home to change into her best clothes, then made her way into the war-torn city centre. Now as the British officer looked at her, she could see his surprise. He was a man of about forty, and something about the expression in his dark-brown eyes made Emer sense that he might be kind.

'May I ask you a question, please?' she said, speaking confidently and clearly, glad for once of her elocution classes.

'Allow me a question first,' replied the officer in what Emer recognised as a cultured English accent. 'What's a young lady like you doing out on your own? The city centre is dangerous.'

'I'm here because … I'm here because I fear for my father's life.'

'Is he an army officer?'

'Yes, sir, he's a captain. But … but not in your army.'

'Ah,' said the man.

'I'm told he was fighting here at City Hall. Can you tell me, please, if he's been captured or wounded, or … or what might have happened to him? His name is Captain Davey.'

The man hesitated, and Emer looked at him appealingly. 'Please, sir, I'm worried sick. I'm asking you, as a gentleman, to help me. I just want to know if he's been taken prisoner.'

The man held her gaze, then nodded almost imperceptibly. He opened the pocket of his tunic and took out a list.

'Davey, you say?'

'Yes, sir, Captain Eamon Davey.'

Emer held her breath as the officer read the list, then he lowered it and looked at her.

'He *was* here.'

'Was?'

'But I'm sorry to have to tell you that he was shot.'

Emer felt like her world was falling apart. 'No!' she cried. 'No …'

'He's not among the dead,' said the man sympathetically. 'He's just listed as wounded.'

'Oh, thank God for that! And … was he badly wounded?'

'I don't have that sort of detail.'

'Do you know where he'd be now?'

'Under guard in hospital, I should think.'

'Which hospital, sir?'

'Afraid I wouldn't know that. But he'll be properly treated. Meanwhile you should get off the streets, miss. This is no place for a girl like you.'

The man went to move off, but Emer called out. 'Sir?'

'Yes?'

'Thank you.'

The officer nodded, then returned to his men.

Emer walked away, her head spinning. It was a relief to know that Dad hadn't been killed. But he was wounded, maybe seriously. Somehow she had to locate his hospital and find out how he was.

'I hate being the bearer of bad tidings,' said Sergeant Kirwan, 'but I promised Jack here I'd let you know one way or the other.'

The family were all in the parlour, with everyone hanging on the words of the policeman from Mr Madigan's station. Jack had been reprimanded for his trip to Kilmainham, but his mother had been so worried to hear that her husband was missing that Jack's cycling to the barracks paled into insignificance.

That had been this morning, and the family had been on edge all day, praying for Da's deliverance and listening to every rumour as Dublin descended into war. Now it was early evening, and martial law had been declared by the government – the British Army officially ruled the city.

'There's no doubt, it was definitely my John who was abducted?' asked Ma, her face ashen.

Sergeant Kirwan nodded solemnly. 'A local who knows him saw John being taken prisoner outside the workhouse. I'm sorry it's taken till now to be able to tell you, but we've only just got the man's statement.'

'Did they injure Da?' asked Maureen.

'No, just marched him off at gunpoint.'

'Into the South Dublin Union?' asked Jack.

'Yes.'

'What are you doing to get him back?' said Mary.

'The army is trying to recapture the grounds. But it's a huge complex, and the rebels are fighting hard. I don't want to mislead you by pretending it'll be easy.'

'So what are you saying?' said Ma, her voice cracking. 'That … that we should prepare for the worst?!'

'No, absolutely not,' said Sergeant Kirwan. 'I know you've heard about Michael Lahiff and James O'Brien being shot. But since then no other DMP men have been killed, and the rebels seem to be acting properly and observing the rules of war. I'm sure they won't mistreat John.'

But with battles raging through the South Dublin Union, he could easily get shot, thought Jack. He half listened as the policeman tried to reassure his family, but his mind was racing. And then a plan formed. He swallowed hard, knowing it would be difficult to pull off – and dangerous. But he couldn't let anything happen to Da. Whatever it took, he had to save him.

'For the love of God, Emer! What the hell got into you?!'

Emer recoiled from the venom of her father's words. He was

205

rarely angry with her and never used language like this. He was lying in a hospital bed on a crowded ward, his wounded leg heavily bandaged and his face pale and drawn. The unexpected harshness of his words, coming after all the fear and uncertainty Emer had felt as she tried to find him, was too much. Unable to stop herself, she burst into tears.

'I'm sorry, Dad,' she sobbed. 'I … I'm sorry.' She slumped down in the chair beside her father's bed, the air heavy with the smell of antiseptic. The ward was busy, with nurses tending to the many patients wounded and injured in the fighting, and nobody paid attention to Emer as she tried to gather herself.

It had been a long, stressful day. It took her hours to find the hospital in which her father was being detained, and she had had to plead with the soldier on guard duty to allow her a few minutes with him. She had been frightened to see her father looking weakened and vulnerable in his hospital bed, and when he snapped at her for staying in Dublin for the Rising, suddenly it all overwhelmed her.

She felt her hand being squeezed now, and through her tear-filled eyes she saw that her father's expression had softened.

'It's all right, love,' he said gently. 'It's all right, don't cry.'

Emer felt better on hearing his words, and she dabbed at her eyes.

'It's a foolish thing you did,' said her father. 'But the reason I was angry is because you mean so much to Mam and me. Do you understand?'

'Yes, Dad.'

'Good girl,' he said, giving her hand another squeeze.

'And, Dad, are you … are you going to be all right?'

'Of course I am. My leg was fractured by a bullet, so I might be left with a bit of a limp, but I'll be grand.' He tried for a grin. 'Sure it's hard to kill a bad thing.'

'But … will they send you to prison, Dad?'

'I don't know, love. I suppose it depends on how the Rising goes.'

'I don't think we're going to win, Dad. Everyone says thousands of British troops are heading for Dublin.'

'Then so be it. But we've made a stand for Ireland, and the whole world will see that. If I'm a prisoner for a while, that's a price we'll pay.'

'Right.'

'But that's enough of a price for our family. You don't get involved again, Emer. Understood?'

'Yes, Dad.'

'So you go home, keep your head down and write to Mam and tell her I'm being looked after. The army will be taking over the trains to move troops, but I'm sure Mam will get back as soon as she can. All right?'

Things weren't really all right, thought Emer: the Volunteers were outnumbered and ultimately doomed, Dad was wounded and a prisoner, and Mam was trapped a hundred and fifty miles away in Ennis. But her father was alive, and he would be easier in his mind if she sounded positive.

'All right, Dad,' she answered brightly. 'All right.'

Jack knocked nervously on the Daveys' front door. Earlier he had met Joan, who told him about Emer's dramatic departure from her mother on the train and about Mr Davey's capture at City Hall. He hoped Emer would be at home now, yet he dreaded asking her the question that he had come to pose.

Biting his lip, he listened intently, then heard footsteps in the hallway. The door was opened by Emer.

'Jack,' she said. He picked up at once on her weary tone and serious expression.

'I need to talk to you,' he said. 'Can I come in for a minute?'

'Of course.' Emer ushered him into the hall and led the way to the kitchen. 'Do you want a glass of milk? I'm just having one.'

'No, thanks,' answered Jack. 'You go ahead.'

Emer indicated for him to join her at the kitchen table, and Jack sat down.

'How's your da?' he asked. 'Joan told me about him being wounded.'

'Bad news travels fast.'

'Well … at least he's alive.'

'Yeah,' agreed Emer. 'His leg is badly injured, but the doctors told him he'll be OK.'

'I'm glad. Because … because things aren't so good with my own da.'

'Oh?'

'Ben and Gladys didn't tell you?'

'No, I haven't seen them. What's happened?'

'Da was taken prisoner. It looks like he's being held by the rebels in the South Dublin Union.'

'God,' said Emer, lowering her untouched glass of milk. 'I'm really sorry to hear that, Jack.'

'Thanks. I wanted … I wanted to ask you a big favour.'

'Anything, Jack.'

'You mightn't say that when you know what it is.'

'So, what is it?'

Jack hesitated, then took the plunge. 'I have to try and get Da out of the Union. The army and the rebels are battling it out there – he could wind up getting killed. But I need your help to do it.'

'What can I do?'

'I want to pretend to be a Fianna runner. It's the only way I could get to Da and try to free him. Will you back my story if I pretend I'm a runner for the rebels?'

Emer looked taken aback. 'Do you … do you know what you're asking, Jack?'

'For you to go against your beliefs. It's an awful thing to ask, and I hate doing it – but Da's life is at stake. I promise I won't involve you any more than I have to. I swear I won't do anything against the rebels, I won't betray them in any way. I just want to get in, free my da, and get out again.'

Jack could see that Emer was in a quandary. He looked her in the eye, then spoke softly again. 'I know it's not fair asking you. But I have to. So, will you help me?'

CHAPTER TWENTY-ONE

The roar of exploding shells carried on the warm morning air as the rebel positions came under a barrage of fire. It was Wednesday, the third day of the Rising, and British artillery based at Trinity College unleashed lethal salvoes, while the gunboat *Helga* had sailed up the River Liffey and was bombarding the city centre. Emer could hear the explosions as she and Jack made their way along James's Street, and she silently gave thanks that her father wasn't on the receiving end of the shellfire raining down upon the rebels.

Dublin was being wrecked, with soldiers and civilians getting killed and maimed, and Emer wondered how she could ever have thought that war could be a glorious thing. She still believed that the Volunteers were brave, and that they were right to fight for Irish freedom. Seeing Dad with his leg shattered, however, and knowing that men on both sides would die agonising deaths, had made her see that warfare was anything but glamorous.

She passed the Guinness brewery, where huge metal boilers were being commandeered by the army, drilled with rifle holes, mounted on wheels and turned into makeshift armoured cars. It was as if normal life had stopped, to be replaced by a world in which everything had been turned on its head. Last night, her own loyalties had been abruptly challenged by Jack's request, and even now, as she walked alongside him, she wasn't certain she was doing the right thing.

Her father had insisted that their family's role in the Rising was over and that she was to keep her head down until Mam got back from Ennis. Yet here she was, making her way with Jack towards the South Dublin Union, where she was going to pretend that he was a fellow rebel and Fianna runner. She trusted Jack when he said he wouldn't betray the rebels in any way, and that he just wanted to rescue his father, but she still felt uncomfortable. It had been really tough to choose between her loyalty to the rebel cause and her loyalty to Jack as a friend. In the end she had been swayed by the memory of her fear for Dad when she heard City Hall had been captured. Clearly Jack felt the same way about his father, and Emer's gut instinct was to help him, even if it meant telling lies to people on the rebel side.

Her thoughts were broken now by a burst of machine-gun fire, and Jack nodded in the direction of the South Dublin Union.

'Getting close,' he said.

'Yeah.'

He stopped and looked at her seriously. 'Are you ready to do this?'

Emer paused, took a deep breath, then nodded. 'Ready as I'll ever be. Let's go.'

Jack dropped from the top of the boundary wall and hit the ground with a thud. The impact sent a wave of pain up through his feet, but he ignored it and turned back to the wall. Emer was poised to drop too, and Jack moved quickly towards where she was likely to land, to catch her and help cushion the fall.

He was hugely grateful to Emer for agreeing to his plan, and he admired the plucky way she had committed herself to the rescue once she overcame her qualms. Now he helped to break her fall as Emer dropped from the wall and landed inside the grounds of the South Dublin Union.

'All right?' he asked.

'Yeah, fine.'

The Union's buildings were spread over a sprawling site between James's Street and Rialto. In addition to the workhouse, there were two churches, various residences, an infirmary, a nurses' home and a bakery. Jack and Emer crouched down low as they got their bearings, the air around them resounding with gunfire.

Jack took in his surroundings carefully. He needed to figure out which areas were in rebel hands, and to discover where Da might be held. And then what? He wasn't sure – his plan only went so far, and after that he would have to improvise. His thoughts were interrupted by a bout of sustained rifle fire. Jack saw British troops in the distance raining a hail of bullets at a tall, grim-looking stone building, from which the rebels were returning rifle and small-arms fire. Presumably the building was a rebel stronghold, and Jack pointed it out to Emer.

'The Volunteers seem to be holed up in there. If we skirt around the boundary wall, we could approach it from the rear.'

'If it's that easy, why aren't the army doing that?'

'Maybe that route can be fired on from another rebel stronghold.'

'Maybe it can be fired on by the army too.'

Jack considered this, then nodded. 'You could be right. But there's fighting all over the place; there's no completely safe way of doing this.'

'No, I suppose not.'

Jack felt a stab of guilt, and he looked his friend in the eye.

'Look, I could go on by myself at this stage, Emer. And you could–'

'No,' she interjected firmly. 'I said I'd help you, and I'm not backing out now.'

'Are you sure?'

'Positive. We're in it together.'

'OK. Let's stay low and skirt the wall then. All right?'

'Yeah.'

Further away in the complex a machine gun opened up, but Jack ignored it and looked at Emer. 'On a count of three?' he said.

'All right.'

'One … two … three!' he counted, then they rose from the ground and sprinted along the perimeter wall.

Emer heard a scream, and she realised that some of the bullets flying through the air had hit their target. The cry came from a low building whose ground-floor windows had all been shattered, but Emer and Jack didn't stop to investigate and instead continued running along the inside of the wall.

She thought of how outraged her father would be if he knew she was putting herself in danger again. But in spite of what Dad had said – and her own unease at tricking his comrades in the Volunteers – she couldn't deny the loyalty she felt towards Jack.

Even if they got safely inside the rebel stronghold, however, there was no guarantee that Mr Madigan would be easily found. In such a large complex as the South Dublin Union, he could be anywhere. *Or he could already be dead.* It was a frightening thought, and she prayed for Jack's sake that his father was alive and well.

They reached a turn in the boundary wall, and Jack halted and dropped down in a crouch. Emer joined him, glad to catch her breath.

'Look,' said Jack, pointing. 'They're going to use bayonets.'

Emer looked across an expanse of open ground and saw a patrol of British soldiers attaching bayonets to their rifles. Clearly they were expecting hand-to-hand fighting, and it brought home to Emer how territory held by both the army and the rebels was in a state of flux. The sooner she and Jack made their move, the better. She turned to him and indicated the building whose rear they were now facing.

'OK, that's where we want to get. Time to become a Fianna runner.'

Emer reached inside her coat and pulled out an old, side-brimmed military hat of her father's that she had found at home. It was the same type of hat as was worn by Fianna members, but it was a little big for Jack, so she pulled it down tight on his head. 'Ready to make a run for it?' she asked, trying to keep the fear from her voice.

'Yeah, the army don't seem to be firing on this side.'

'OK, then. Let's do it!'

☣ ☣ ☣

Jack ran flat out, not wanting to be exposed in the open for a second longer than he had to be. He could hear Emer sprinting right on his heels as they made for the rear door of the grim stone building. 'Fianna despatches!' he cried out loudly. 'Don't shoot, Fianna despatches!'

Jack and Emer reached the door, and he immediately tried the handle. The door was locked, and Jack pounded on it and again called out, 'Fianna despatches, don't shoot!'

There was movement at a nearby window, then he heard a shouted command. The bolt of the door was loudly undone, and it swung open.

'Where the hell did you come from?!' asked a red-haired man with thick stubble on his chin. He was dressed in a soiled

Volunteer's uniform and held a Mauser pistol that was pointed at Jack.

'We're runners from HQ! Let us in before we're shot!' cried Jack.

The man ushered them in, and immediately they encountered another Volunteer – an older man carrying a rifle that was trained on Jack's chest.

Jack had decided that the best way to carry off his deception was to sound completely confident, and to behave as though his presence here was entirely plausible. 'You can lower the rifle. It's enough being shot at by the Tommies!'

The man slowly lowered the weapon but looked quizzically at Jack. 'What's she doing here?' he asked, indicating Emer.

'I'm from this area,' she answered. 'I know every back lane, so I offered to be a runner.'

The man raised an eyebrow, but Jack was pleased that Emer was following his lead by responding confidently. 'You needn't look down your nose!' she said. 'I've been risking my life since Monday!'

'Sorry ...' said the man slightly sheepishly.

Jack decided to go for broke while they seemed to have the upper hand. 'Where's the police prisoner being held?'

'Why do you ask?' queried the red-haired man.

'We've orders about him from Padraig Pearse,' answered Jack, reasoning that the name of the commanding officer of the Volunteers would carry some weight.

'Yeah?' said the older man.

'Yeah. Where can we find him?'

'He's in the annexe. It's a white-roofed building in behind the next block,' said the man, indicating the direction.

Jack felt a surge of elation. 'Right,' he replied.

'The Tommies are trying to take that area. You want to be really careful.'

'We will,' answered Emer.

'OK, let's go then,' said Jack. 'Thanks for your help,' he added to the two men as he turned for the door.

'Not so fast, son.'

Jack thought that he had carried off the deception, but the red-haired man's words chilled him. He looked around, praying that his fear wasn't obvious. There was no telling what these men might do if they discovered he was on the side of the enemy, but if he dwelt on that he would lose his nerve. 'What is it?' he asked, trying to keep his voice casual.

The red-haired man looked him in the eye. 'We've been pinned down here for nearly two days. What's the latest news from the city?'

Jack was glad that the man wasn't suspicious after all, but he made sure to hide his relief. 'Mixed news,' he said. 'The army retook City Hall, and they've artillery at Phibsboro and Trinity College. But we're holding out in the Four Courts and the Mendicity Institute, so they can't get their reinforcements down the quays.'

'And the troops that landed in Kingstown are pinned down at Mount Street Bridge,' said Emer, 'so the fight goes on!'

Jack didn't want to delay any further, and he thought this was a good note on which to depart. 'So, up the Republic!' he said.

'Up the Republic!' answered the Volunteers, as Jack and Emer made for the door.

The blast of detonating grenades could be heard from nearby, but Emer tried not to flinch in front of the battle-hardened rebels. She was inside the annexe with Jack now, having persuaded its defenders that they were Fianna runners with an important message to deliver.

'Where's Commandant Ceannt?' asked Emer briskly, wanting to give the impression that they had official business with the officer in charge of the Volunteers in the South Dublin Union. While visiting her father in hospital last night, she had discovered that Eamonn Ceannt, one of the signatories to the proclamation of independence, was leading the rebels here, and she hoped that her confident use of his name would make herself and Jack seem credible as Fianna runners.

Most of the Volunteers here were manning sandbag-filled windows, from which they unleashed rifle fire. Two rebels had let her and Jack in, a gaunt youth of about twenty, who Emer suspected was struggling to mask his fear, and a more aggressive, stocky man in his forties who now asked her suspiciously, 'What's it to you where Commandant Ceannt is?'

'We need to know if he's still in command,' answered Jack. 'We've orders from HQ.'

'Yes, he's still in command,' replied the stocky man.

'But he's not here. He's up at the Rialto gate,' added his younger companion.

'Doesn't really matter,' said Emer. 'Our orders are to bring a message for the DMP prisoner. Is he still here?'

'He's down the corridor,' said the youth.

'What the hell are you doing bringing a message for a copper?' asked the stocky man.

'Padraig Pearse is allowing the prisoner to receive a letter from his family,' said Jack.

'What?!' exclaimed the older rebel.

'Pearse wants to show that the Volunteers are behaving properly,' explained Emer. 'So he's letting the prisoner have a letter. That way his family knows he's being treated well.'

Emer found herself holding her breath as the stocky man considered her answer. More grenades exploded nearby. Emer tried not to react too much to the explosions, but prayed instead that the man would swallow their story.

'All right,' he said finally. 'Though it's more than the English would do for us.'

Emer felt a flood of relief, but before she could respond the man spoke again.

'Give me the letter, and I'll get it to him.'

'Sorry,' said Jack, 'but our orders are to give it to him personally.'

Emer was impressed with Jack's quick thinking. Suddenly a hail of bullets thudded into the sandbag at the nearest window.

'You've enough to do here,' said Jack. 'Just tell us where he is, and we'll go there.'

'Bring them to the prisoner, Sean, and don't dilly-dally!' said the stocky man, before picking up his rifle and going to the window.

'OK,' said the youth importantly, 'follow me!'

Jack saw the amazement in his father's eyes. He quickly raised a finger to his lips, hoping that Da wouldn't call out his name. They were in a small storage room down the corridor from where the other Volunteers were exchanging rifle fire with the British troops. Jack knew that Emer was deliberately trying to distract the young Volunteer who had escorted them here. He took advantage of being behind the youth to raise his fingers to his lips again and mime urgently to Da not to give the game away.

To Jack's relief his father gave a tiny nod to indicate that he got the message. Da looked unharmed, but the bad news was that although he was seated in a chair, his wrist was handcuffed and attached to a radiator via a chain. The sound of gunfire and exploding grenades was getting louder all the time, and before Jack could improvise his next move, a loud blast from outside shattered the room's only window. Fragments of glass flew in all directions, and Jack instinctively shielded his face and turned away.

The young Volunteer had been nearest to the window, and blood flowed down his cheek from a deep cut over his eyebrow. He raised his hand to the wound, and immediately it was covered in crimson blood. The youth had looked frightened to begin with, and Jack saw that now he was in shock.

'We need to get you to a medic,' said Emer, and Jack admired his friend's speed in taking advantage of the situation.

'We've no medics here,' said the youth.

'To be bandaged then. Have you first-aid supplies somewhere?'

'Back in the command room.'

'Leave them to sort out the letter,' said Emer, indicating Jack and his father. 'Let's get you back there before you lose any more blood!'

'All right,' said the youth shakily.

Jack could have hugged Emer for her inventiveness, but instead he moved towards Da as his friend helped the young Volunteer out the door.

'What are you doing here, Jack?' asked his father.

'I came to free you!'

'How did you get here?'

'They think we're Fianna runners. I'll explain later – we haven't time now! Where's the key to this chain?'

'With a pile of other keys in the drawer of that press,' said Da, indicating a tall wooden cabinet against the far wall.

Jack quickly crossed the room and pulled open the drawer. To his dismay there were dozens of keys, some on rings, others loose in the bottom of the drawer. 'There's loads! How do we know which it is?' he cried, a hint of panic creeping into his voice. The fighting was getting ever nearer, and now black smoke was wafting in through the broken window. Most worrying of all was the fact that at any moment the injured Volunteer or one of his comrades might come back.

'It's a squat silver key,' said Da.

Jack frantically sorted through the keys, but he didn't see one that fitted this description. 'I can't see it!'

'OK,' said Da, 'pull the whole drawer out and bring it over here!'

Jack grabbed the handle of the drawer and pulled, but it was stiff and it resisted his efforts. He tried again and fought against panic when it wouldn't budge. He gave one final jerk, putting all his strength into it, and this time the drawer suddenly came free. Some of the keys fell out onto the floor, but Jack quickly scooped them up, then ran across the room and laid the drawer before his father. 'Right, which one is it?!'

Emer could feel her heart thumping, but she tried to look cool. It was frightening each time a grenade exploded, but even more terrifying was the thought of being caught trying to free Mr Madigan and treated as spies.

The injured Volunteer was now being bandaged by one of the

other rebels. The stocky man turned to Emer, his expression quizzical. 'Why hasn't your friend delivered the letter by now?' he asked.

Emer tried desperately to think up something that would buy time for Jack to free his father. 'I'm sure he has,' she improvised, 'but Padraig Pearse said the prisoner could write a reply to his family, so he's probably doing that.'

'This is a war zone. We need to get you out of here. Come on!'

'It's all right,' said Emer. 'I'm OK about it. Let's give them time to write something.'

'I'm not OK about it,' said the man, 'and I don't take orders from you. Now shift yourself!'

Emer realised that arguing further would only make him suspicious, so instead she moved as slowly as possible towards the door. She followed the man out into the corridor, dreading to think what would happen when they reached the room containing Mr Madigan.

Jack turned the key in the lock, and the handcuffs clicked open. He watched as Da swiftly pulled the manacle off his wrist and felt a surge of elation when his father smiled and rose from the chair. Just then the door opened and Emer entered, closely followed by the stocky Volunteer. The man had his rifle hung over his shoulder, but when he saw his prisoner unchained, he immediately unslung the weapon and aimed it at Da.

'Don't shoot!' cried Jack. 'Don't shoot an unarmed man!' The Volunteer looked furious, and Jack felt sick with fear that he would kill Da for trying to escape. 'Please, it would be murder!'

For a moment everything seemed to hang in the balance, then the man breathed out, and Jack realised that he wasn't going to shoot. Instead the rebel vented his anger by turning on Emer and slapping her hard across the face.

'Lying little bitch!' he cried.

Emer fell back, and instinctively both Jack and his father moved towards the Volunteer.

'Go on,' said the man, 'just give me a reason.'

'Steady, son,' said Da, and Jack controlled his anger. 'Are you all right, Emer?' he added.

'Yeah, I'm fine,' she answered.

'You won't be fine!' snapped the man. 'Spies get shot, and you two came here posing as Fianna.'

Jack felt his stomach tighten. But just then there was a deafening blast as a grenade exploded outside the window. Jack was thrown backwards by the shock wave, and he smacked his shoulder against the wall. His father, however, was a big man weighing fifteen stone, and from the corner of his eye Jack saw that Da had weathered the blast. More than that, Da now sprang forward with surprising agility and clattered into the Volunteer, knocking the rifle from his hand. The rebel tried to fight back, but Jack's father unleashed a pile-driver of a punch that poleaxed the man and left him unconscious on the floor. Jack looked around to see how

Emer was, and his joy suddenly turned to fear as he saw her lying, unmoving, against the wall.

'Bayonet charge!' roared a voice nearby. 'Bayonet charge!'

Thuds of doors being kicked in and screams from men fighting hand-to-hand resounded through the air. Shakily coming to, Emer sat up gingerly. She saw the stocky rebel lying out cold on the ground, and her spirits rose.

'Jack, lock the door!' cried Mr Madigan, then he turned to Emer. 'Are you OK?'

'Yes,' she answered. She felt a bit bruised from the blast, which had thrown her against the wall, but otherwise she was unhurt. 'What happened him?' she asked, pointing at the unconscious rebel.

'Da levelled him!' said Jack.

Mr Madigan smiled and offered Emer his hand, and she rose to her feet. Now that her head was clearing, she understood Jack's father wanting to lock the door to keep the rebels at bay. But the sooner they made their escape, the better, so she pointed towards the far end of the annexe. 'If we head down the corridor and out the back of the building, that should take us away from the worst of the fighting,' she said.

'All right,' said Mr Madigan. 'And thanks, Emer, I'll never forget this.'

Emer gave a wry smile. 'Thank me when we're out.'

'Da, what are you doing?' asked Jack, as Mr Madigan took the handcuffs and bound the wrists of the unconscious rebel behind his back.

'I'm arresting this fella. I'll sling him over my shoulder and take him with us.'

'No, Da, you can't!' said Jack.

'This man killed two British soldiers. I heard him boasting about it. I'm not letting him away with murder.'

'But he's a soldier at war – that's how he'd see it. Leave him here, Da, please. He can be captured with the others.'

'Or he could escape scot-free.'

'We're the ones who need to escape, Da. And you couldn't escape if Emer hadn't risked everything coming here.'

'And I'm really grateful, Emer.'

'Then leave this man behind, Mr Madigan,' pleaded Emer.

'I can't. It's my duty.'

'You've a duty to Emer, Da! Even though her father's wounded in hospital, she went against the rebels for you. When this is over, you can't tell anyone what she did. And it'll all come out if you arrest this man.'

'It's true, Mr Madigan,' said Emer. 'If it ever comes out that I changed sides, I'd be seen as a traitor. And probably my Dad too. Please don't do that to us – we could be shot by our own side.'

Jack's father said nothing for a moment, and Emer prayed that he wouldn't ignore her plea.

'Emer, I ... I'm sorry,' he answered. 'I wasn't thinking straight.

This fella can stay behind,' he added, indicating the rebel, 'so let's get out of here.'

'Thanks, Mr Madigan,' Emer said.

The policeman nodded in reply, then stopped to pick up the Volunteer's discarded rifle.

'Can we leave the rifle, Da?' suggested Jack. 'If we're armed, both sides could end up shooting at us. Emer has a better idea.'

'What's that?'

Emer reached into her pocket and took out three homemade Red Cross armbands. 'If you take off your tunic, Mr Madigan, you'll look less like a policeman. And if we all put these on our arms, we can pretend we're Red Cross.'

'I'm not sure that will fool anyone,' said the policeman dubiously.

'It mightn't fool them up close,' said Jack, 'but it could buy us a second's doubt if someone is going to take a potshot. That could make the difference.'

Mr Madigan nodded again. 'All right.'

He slipped off his tunic, Jack took off his military hat, and Emer quickly distributed the armbands. The sounds of battle were raging outside, but she steeled herself for what was ahead.

'Ready?' asked Mr Madigan.

'Yeah,' Emer said. 'Let's go!'

Black smoke hung in the air, and Jack coughed as it stung his lungs. The burning smell was horrible, but he was grateful for the smoke, which hampered visibility as they ran down the corridor of the annexe. He heard shouts and screams behind them, and all around were the sounds of rifle shots and small-arms fire, but Jack, his father and Emer didn't stop running until they reached the end of the long corridor.

'Take one end of this!' cried Da, grabbing a discarded stretcher that was propped inside the rear door of the building. 'I'll take the other end, and we'll run like we're stretcher bearers! Emer, you open the door for us.'

'OK!'

Jack took hold of the stretcher's handles as Emer opened the door and looked cautiously out into the sunlight. 'All clear?' he asked.

'I think so,' she answered. 'Let's make for the wall again!'

Emer began running, crouched low to be less of a target, and Jack and his father raced after her, also staying low. Jack's heart pounded painfully, and it wasn't just from exertion – there was a real risk here of stopping a bullet. They had been lucky to escape the confusion of the annexe, but to hope to reach the boundary wall unseen was asking a lot. Sure enough, after they had run about twenty yards, a shot rang out and a bullet ricocheted off the cobblestones behind them.

'Stretcher bearers, don't shoot!' cried Jack. 'Stretcher bearers!'

Jack and his father continued racing behind Emer towards the shelter offered by the corner of a nearby building. Just then a voice cried out, 'It's the copper! Open fire, it's the copper!'

Jack had the rear of the stretcher, and he urged his father to greater speed as a volley of shots rang out. The corner was drawing near, but the final yards seemed to take an eternity to cover. Jack prayed that the riflemen wouldn't be accurate enough to hit rapidly moving targets, but he still felt horribly exposed.

Emer rounded the side of the building a couple of paces ahead of him, then more shots rang out. Da cried out and fell, and Jack tripped over him, the momentum bringing him around the corner. Immediately he rolled over on the ground and looked back, terrified of what he might find.

His father was sprawled out right at the corner. He was clasping his ankle, and there was blood on his hand. Jack reached out and grabbed his arm to pull him to safety. Emer suddenly materialised, and Jack realised that she had come back to help. She grabbed Mr Madigan's other leg, and they pulled him unceremoniously around the corner, just as more shots kicked off the nearby cobblestones.

'Are you all right, Da?' asked Jack.

'Yeah. Yeah, I'm lucky, it's just a graze.'

'Are you sure?' asked Emer.

Jack watched with relief as his father tried putting weight on his ankle and rose with just a grimace.

'I'm all right,' said Da. 'Let's get moving!'

'What about the stretcher?' said Jack.

'Too risky reaching round for it! Let's just make a run for the wall!'

They ran off again, keeping low to the ground, and Jack felt more anxious than ever. It would be unbearable to fall at the last hurdle, having got this close to freedom, yet it could easily happen.

They covered the ground at speed, then rounded another corner and suddenly came face to face with a British patrol. The solders immediately aimed their rifles, their evil-looking bayonets glistening in the sun.

'Don't shoot!' screamed Emer. 'Don't shoot!'

'We're not rebels!' said Jack. 'Don't shoot!'

'Who the hell *are* you?' demanded their officer, his pistol pointed at Da's chest.

'I'm Sergeant John Madigan, Dublin Metropolitan Police,' said Da. 'I've just escaped two days' captivity by the rebels.'

'Why are you wearing Red Cross armbands?'

'To try and confuse rebel gunmen while we escaped. You can see this is the rest of my uniform. And this is my warrant card,' said Da, handing the officer his police identification.

To Jack's relief the officer relaxed.

'Well, I'll be damned!' he said, holstering his weapon. 'Lower the rifles, men,' he instructed, and the soldiers lowered their weapons, while still keeping them at the ready.

'And who would these be?' asked the officer, indicating Jack and Emer.

'Two very brave youngsters who helped me escape. This is my son, Jack Madigan.'

'Good lad, Jack,' said the officer.

In spite of everything that had happened, Jack found himself smiling. 'Thank you, sir.'

'And Jack's friend …'

Jack saw his father hesitate for a second as he indicated Emer. 'The very brave Mary Murphy.'

Jack had to hold back a grin. He was pleased that Da was keeping his word and ensuring there would be no mention of a girl called Emer Davey in this story.

'Well done, Mary,' said the officer.

'Thank you,' answered Emer politely.

'I take it we're in army-held territory now?' said Da.

'In this part of the grounds, yes,' replied the officer. 'Still fighting tooth and nail in other parts, but from here over to the side entrance is all in our hands. Your ordeal is over.'

Da tied a clean handkerchief around his grazed ankle, and Jack sighed, the tension of the last few days finally easing. He suddenly felt drained. His father turned and looked at him, then held his arms open like he used to do when Jack was small. Without a second's hesitation, Jack buried himself in his father's arms and hugged him hard.

'Jack,' said Da, 'you're … you're a son in a million …'

To Jack's surprise there were tears in his father's eyes. And in an instant his own eyes welled up as his pent-up emotions were released. 'You're one in a million too, Da,' he said. 'You're one in a million too.'

'And let's not forget this young lady,' said Da after a moment, as he gently unfolded himself from Jack's embrace.

He offered Emer his hand, which she shook. 'Thank you with all of my heart,' he said.

'I'm just delighted you're OK,' she answered with a smile.

Jack turned to his friend and offered her his hand also. 'I don't know what to say …'

Suddenly a handshake seemed inadequate, and he reached out and hugged Emer. 'You're a star,' he said. 'You're just a star!'

Emer hugged him back. 'Thanks, Jack,' she answered softly, then she grinned. 'And you're not too bad yourself!'

Jack thought she was the best friend anyone could ever have, and he gave her arm a final squeeze, then turned to his father.

'Time to go home, I think,' said Da.

'Yes,' said Jack with a smile. 'Time to go home.'

CHAPTER TWENTY-TWO

Emer loved the sound of Sunday-morning church bells chiming across the city, but today she only half heard them as she sat beside her father's hospital bed. She could see the strain in his face, and she suspected that he was in pain, even though he was putting on a good front for herself and Mam.

Her mother had managed to get back from Ennis on Wednesday night, and she had been furious with Emer for tricking her and staying on in Dublin. But Emer understood that her mother's anger was fuelled by love, and within moments of being reunited, the anger was replaced by relief, with both of them tearfully embracing. Even so she had told neither of her parents about her adventure in rescuing Mr Madigan, and she was confident that Jack and his father would never reveal the secret of her involvement.

It was six days now since the Rising had begun. Last night the rebels had finally been forced to surrender to the overwhelmingly large British forces. The centre of Dublin was wrecked, hundreds of people had been killed and injured, and Emer found herself wondering if it had been worth it. It was generally felt that the rebels had fought bravely, but most people in Dublin were unsympathetic to the Rising, and many were horrified by what they saw as pointless death and destruction.

A bell rang on the ward to signal the end of the strictly enforced visiting time, and Emer reached out and held her father's hand. 'Mind yourself, Dad. And I'll keep praying that you get better.'

'Good girl,' he said. 'Give your dad a kiss,' he added, offering his cheek.

Emer reached out and kissed him, then stood up as her mother did the same.

'I meant to say, Molly, you might re-open the shops,' suggested Dad.

'You're definitely on the mend when you're thinking about business,' Emer's mother answered with a smile. 'But you're right, we should try to get back to normal.'

'Whatever that will be ...' said Dad with a hint of sadness.

Emer felt a surge of affection for him, and on impulse she reached over and kissed him on the cheek again. 'See you tomorrow, Dad.'

'Bye, pet.'

Emer waved, then walked with her mother down the sunlit ward towards the exit.

She and Mam tried to be cheerful on their hospital visits, but the future was far from certain, and Emer's belief in the rebellion had been shaken by all the pain and destruction she had witnessed in the past week. In spite of his shattered leg, Dad still believed that he had done the right thing for Ireland, and he insisted that the Irish nation was entitled to win its freedom by force of arms. Emer believed in freedom and admired people like Dad who were prepared to suffer for their ideals. But dying for Ireland didn't seem quite so noble now, and living a good life and being loyal to friends seemed more important.

She walked down the stairs with her mother, the hospital smells of antiseptic and floor polish heavy in the air. The events of the past week swirled through her head. Although the Rising had failed and Dad was a prisoner, at least he was still alive. And despite whatever sentence he would have to serve, in time they would be together again as a family. She was glad, too, that through her help Jack and his family were reunited. Because if she had learnt anything in the dramas of recent days, it was that family and friends were what mattered most.

They reached the exit door of the hospital. Mam must have seen that she was lost in her thoughts, because she turned to her and spoke reassuringly. 'Don't worry too much, love. We're going to be all right. It'll work out in the end.'

Emer smiled at her mother. There was no telling what the future would bring – either for Ireland, or for the ruined city of Dublin, or for Jack, or Gladys, or Ben, or Joan, or any of them. But whatever it brought, they would face it together and make the best of it. 'You're right, Mam,' she said. 'We *are* going to be all right.' Then she took her mother's hand and they walked out together into the warm spring sunshine.

EPILOGUE

Mr Madigan continued serving as a policeman after the DMP was absorbed into An Garda Síochána, the police force of the new Irish Free State. He always played down his captivity during the Rising, however, and never revealed Emer's role in his rescue.

Mrs Madigan worked on as a milliner, and the family lived on Ellesmere Avenue for many years.

Jack's boyhood dream of being a detective never came to pass. Instead he changed plans and moved to London, where he had a long and successful career with the BBC, in the new medium of radio.

Gerry left school at thirteen and worked on the horse and cart with his uncle, then emigrated to New Zealand, where he made a new life as a horse breeder.

Joan worked in an office before meeting an American naval officer. She married him and raised a family in San Diego, in a house she nostalgically named 'Tolka Fields'.

Ben didn't become a professional cricketer but followed his father into the family's successful electrical business. Gladys surprised no-one by continuing to be a model student; she eventually became vice principal of her old school.

Phelim O'Connell remained an ardent nationalist and was killed at the age of eighteen, as a gunman during the Irish Civil War.

Brother McGill was devastated by Phelim's untimely death. Thereafter he avoided discussing politics with his pupils.

Miss Clarke resigned after a row with Sister Assumpta. She returned to her native Hoylake, where she continued working as a teacher.

Mrs Davey and Emer kept the family grocery business going during Mr Davey's imprisonment following the Rising; the business would eventually expand to five shops. Mr Davey recovered from his injury, but he was left with a limp in his wounded leg. He played no further active role in the War of Independence but stayed interested in politics, and in later years he served for a time on Dublin Corporation.

Emer studied commerce and helped to run, and eventually manage, the family's grocery shops. She married a classmate of Ben's, exchanged Christmas cards every year with Jack, and remained friends with Gladys for the rest of her life. She never told anyone of her role in Mr Madigan's rescue, and until they died, she and Jack remembered it with pride – but kept it as their own private secret.

HISTORICAL NOTE

The Easter Rising of 1916 took place primarily in Dublin and lasted for six days. Heavily outnumbered, and with defeat inevitable, Padraig Pearse signed a general surrender to prevent further bloodshed. By that stage huge damage had been done to central Dublin by artillery fire, and over two thousand civilians had been wounded. Total casualties on all sides came to more than four hundred people dead, and over half of those were civilians.

Because of the loss of life and the damage to the city – and also because many Dubliners had family members serving with the British Army in the First World War – the mood of the citizens of Dublin was generally unsympathetic to the rebels.

That hostility changed, however, after the British Army Commander, General John Maxwell, oversaw the execution of rebel leaders – including Eamonn Ceannt, the Commander at the South Dublin Union, and the seriously wounded James Connolly, who had to be carried in on a stretcher for his execution by firing squad. This mood shift led to the rise of the Sinn Féin political party, and following a bloody guerrilla campaign, twenty-six of the thirty-two counties of Ireland gained independence as the Irish Free State in January 1922.

The First World War raged from 1914 to 1918 and was fought

by the British Empire, the French Empire and their allies, against Germany, the Austro-Hungarian Empire and Turkey. Conscription for the war was successfully resisted in Ireland, but over 200,000 Irishmen are thought to have fought on the Allied side. The First World War marked the beginning of highly mechanised warfare, and casualty rates were appalling, with more than sixteen million people estimated to have died due to the conflict.

Friend or Foe is a work of fiction, and the families of Jack, Emer, Gladys and Ben, Joan and Gerry are figments of my imagination. The historical events described are real, however, and the skirmish with the Lancers, the city-centre looting, the shelling by the gun-boat *Helga* and the recapturing of City Hall were all actual events.

Gerry's cottage is fictitious, but the River Tolka was a popular swimming spot, and the area described in the book is now part of the Tolka Valley Park.

Monasterevin is still a magical interconnection of waterways. Although cargo hasn't been transported on the canal there for many years, the warehouses that Jack saw remain standing today.

The workhouse complex of the South Dublin Union, where Jack and Emer carry out the rescue of Mr Madigan, is now the site of St James's Hospital. Other locations such as the city cattle market and Tara Street Baths have been built upon since 1916, but Ellesmere Avenue is a real place, and the streets where Emer and her friends lived are little changed.

Brian Gallagher,
Dublin, 2015.

BRIAN GALLAGHER was born in Dublin. He is a full-time writer whose plays and short stories have been produced in Ireland, Britain and Canada. He has worked extensively in radio and television, writing many dramas and documentaries. Brian collaborated with composer Shaun Purcell on the musical *Larkin*, for which he wrote the book and lyrics, and on *Winds of Change* for RTÉ's Lyric FM. His latest show is *Whiskey in the Jar*, a musical for which he wrote the book and lyrics, with music by Dave 'Doc' O'Connor.

Brian is the author of four adult novels, and his other books of historical fiction for young readers are *Across the Divide*, set during the 1913 Dublin Lockout; *Taking Sides*, which takes place against the backdrop of the Civil War; *Secrets and Shadows*, a spy novel that begins with the North Strand bombings during World War 2; and *Stormclouds*, set in Northern Ireland during the turbulent summer of 1969. He lives with his family in Dublin.

Praise for Brian Gallagher's other books:

Across the ░░░░

'The atmosphere of a troubled city awash with tension and poverty is excellently captured.' *Irish Examiner*

'A compelling historical novel.' *Inis Magazine*

'Highly recommended.' *Bookfest*

Taking Sides

'An involving, exciting read.' *Carousel Magazine*

'Gripping right from its first page … Dramatic action and storytelling skill.' *Evening Echo*

'Riveting.' *Sunday Independent*

Secrets and Shadows

'Heart-stopping action likely to hold readers aged nine to teens in its thrall.' *Evening Echo*

'Weav[es] historic fact and period detail into a fictional but nevertheless entirely credible story … Nail-biting.' *Books Ireland*

Stormclouds

'Just beautiful writing.' *Sunday Independent*

'Thoroughly researched historical fiction.' *Inis Magazine*

'This accurate depiction of violence … will surprise and educate many. A worthy accomplishment.' *Kirkus Reviews*